Arthur Annesley Ronald Firbank was born in 1886, a grandson of Joseph Firbank, a Durham miner who later amassed a fortune as a railway contractor. His mother, to whom he was greatly attached, was an Irishwoman of considerable beauty and cultivated tastes. Owing to a weak constitution, Firbank was educated mainly at home; in 1906 he went up to Trinity Hall, Cambridge, where he was received into the Roman Catholic Church.

Until 1914 Firbank travelled a good deal but lived mainly in London, habitué of the Café Royal, well-known for his extreme and deliberate aestheticism, his sinuous, loosely-jointed figure, and his morbid nervousness, which issued in hysterical laughter in an elaborately capricious manner. The First World War was spent in retreat in Oxford; then again until his death in Rome in 1926 he travelled widely.

Firbank's first work was published in 1905, a volume of two short stories, *Odette d'Antrevernes* and *A Study in Temperament*. Ten years later Grant Richards brought out his first novel, *Vainglory*. The following were published later, all initially at the author's own expense: *Inclinations* (1916); *Caprice* (1917); *Valmouth* (1919); *The Princess Zoubaroff*, a play (1920); *Santal* (1921); *The Flower beneath the Foot* (1923); *Prancing Nigger* (1924 – published in England in 1925 under Firbank's original title, *Sorrow in Sunlight*); *Concerning the Eccentricities of Cardinal Pirelli* (1926). *The Artificial Princess* (1934) appeared posthumously; it had been written before *Vainglory* but put away and forgotten by the author.

Ronald Firbank

THE FLOWER
BENEATH THE FOOT

With an Introduction by
John Mortimer

Penguin Books

Penguin Books Ltd, Harmondsworth, Middlesex, England
Viking Penguin Inc., 40 West 23rd Street, New York, New York 10010, U.S.A.
Penguin Books Australia Ltd, Ringwood, Victoria, Australia
Penguin Books Canada Ltd, 2801 John Street, Markham, Ontario, Canada L3R 1B4
Penguin Books (N.Z.) Ltd, 182–190 Wairau Road, Auckland 10, New Zealand

First published 1923
New Edition published by Duckworth 1929
Published in Penguin Books 1986

Introduction copyright © John Mortimer, 1986
All rights reserved

Made and printed in Great Britain by
Hazell Watson & Viney Ltd,
Member of BPCC Group,
Aylesbury, Bucks
Filmset in Linotron Aldus by
Rowland Phototypesetting Ltd
Bury St Edmunds, Suffolk

INTRODUCTION
by John Mortimer

Here are three masters of twentieth-century dialogue at work, using speech which is not merely there to push along a story but is an end in itself, syncopated, funny and full of unusual rhythms. The reader is no longer following an argument but is half hearing an eccentric conversation across a crowded room. And yet the lines are perfectly placed and the authors' interjections are just sufficient to set the scene.

*

'Probably a creature with a whole gruesome family?' she indirectly inquired.

'Unhappily he's only just left Oxford.'

'Ah, handsome, then. I hope.'

'On the contrary, he's like one of those cherubs one sees on eighteenth-century fonts with their mouths stuffed with cake.'

'Not *really*.'

'And he wears glasses.'

'But he takes them off sometimes?'

'That's just what I don't know.'

*

'I say Bertie,' he said after a pause of about an hour and a quarter.

'Hallo?'

'Do you like the name Mabel?'

'No.'

'No?'

'No.'

'You don't think there's a kind of music in the word like the wind gently rustling through the tree tops?'

'No.'

He seemed disappointed for a moment; then he cheered up.

'Of course you wouldn't. You were always a fat-headed worm without a soul, weren't you?'

*

'Who is that very important young man?' asked Mrs Blackwater of Lady Throbbing.

'I don't know, dear. He bowed to *you*.'

'How very nice . . . I wasn't quite sure . . . He reminds me a little of Prince A—.'

'It's so nice in these days, isn't it dearest, to see someone who really looks . . . don't you think?'

'You mean the beard?'

'*The beard among other things*, darling.'

*

The second and third quotations are from novelists, P. G. Wodehouse and Evelyn Waugh, who achieved great popular success. The first is by one who remains a specialized taste and, perhaps, a minority enthusiasm. As long ago as 1929 in the magazine *Life and Letters* Waugh paid his generous tribute to Ronald Firbank. Almost sixty years after his death Firbank lives on, not only in his books, but in the work of his successors trying to write comic, articulate and original English fiction.

Firbank isn't simply a literary curiosity, a bridge between *The Importance of Being Earnest* and *Vile Bodies*, a link between Aubrey Beardsley and Angela Carter. His books are full of energy and imaginative power. If the test of a novelist is to see whether he creates a world of his own, Firbank passes with a salute of waved parasols and fluttered Benedictions. His entirely modern significance may be judged by a fragment of dialogue from *Caprice*, which he wrote in 1917, and which went laughing on to find its curious echoes in the Theatre of the Absurd. Listen to this for a moment.

'Can you tell how I should go to Croydon?' she asked. The words came slowly, sadly almost.

'To Croydon?'

'You can't go to Croydon.'

'Why not?'

The young man of the whiskers looked amused.

'When we all go to Spain to visit Velazquez –'

'Goya –'

'Velazquez!'

'Goya! Goya! Goya!'

'. . . We'll set you on your way.'

'Goose!'

'One goes to Croydon best by Underground,' the pale looking girl remarked.

Miss Sinquier winced.

*

Great-grandfather Firbank was a Durham miner, who could neither read nor write, and his son Joseph began work down the pit at the age of seven. Later Joseph became a construction worker and, such was the unexpected mobility of Victorian society, an enormously rich railway tycoon. He was a short, rotund man, with the astute eyes and full lips of his grandson, who kept his Durham accent and was given to such words of wisdom as, 'I values at nowt what I gets for nowt.' His son, Sir Thomas Firbank, became a Member of Parliament and married the beautiful and artistic daughter of an Irish clergyman. From these parents Arthur Annesley Ronald was born in 1886, the year of his grandfather's death. So it had taken only a short period of history for the miner's stock to produce a nervous novelist whose imagination flitted around the courts of make-believe kingdoms, the palaces of delinquent cardinals and cathedral closes, worlds as intricately and comically imagined as those of the Drones Club or the Bright Young Things surrounding Lady Metroland. Sitting in the Café Royal he would accuse Osbert Sitwell of having said that the Firbank fortune was founded on boot buttons. Ronald Firbank would rehearse his evidence in a fantastic

7

libel action, laughing nervously, stammering a little and moving his hands rhythmically round his head. 'Look at my hands, my lord,' he would say to the judge. 'How could my father have made boot buttons? No, never! He made the most *wonderful* railways!'

For all his apparent preciosity, and his rooms filled with flowers, Gothic religious figures, gilded candelabras and champagne, where he sat wearing a Chinese jade ring under a large portrait of his mother in court dress, Firbank seems to have retained some of the toughness of his grandfather Joseph. His writing is totally unsentimental and his grasp of the slithering, elusive world of his imagination is ruthlessly consistent. He died at the age of thirty-nine, having produced ten novels and a play which, in spite of his genius for dialogue, lacks the necessary narrative drive for a stage piece.

He seems to have been a sweet-natured, vague and excitable man, whose homosexuality no doubt led to a great deal of unhappiness and frustration: accounts of his life give no hint of real love affairs and he sadly said, 'I can buy companionship.' For most of his life the critics and the public ignored his books, and when he gave a dinner party in an attempt to woo the reviewers he sank under the table, overcome with nerves and champagne, and none of his guests quite understood why they had been invited. At the end of his life a friend wrote that Firbank, of all people, cared least whether he was alive or dead.

Much of his time seems to have been spent seated in the Café Royal, where a writer, Holt Marvell, described him:

> He was truly a habitué of that faded, jaded room. Somedays he sat from noon until midnight in his accustomed seat – to the right as you swing through the door. A thin man with a black felt hat. A narrow man and restless – writhing like a basket of serpents. Clutching at the lapel of his coat, dipping his head like an embarrassed governess. Always paying for drinks. It was he who gave me the life story of the lavatory attendant at the Café, whose children were never told about their father's profession until they were sixteen and old enough to know the facts of life.

Another of Firbank's haunts was the old Eiffel Tower restaurant in Tottenham Court Road. It was there he met the Vorticist painters and Augustus John, who did several drawings of him. He would sit from lunch time till midnight consuming so little that the proprietor was extremely relieved when he ate a whole piece of toast with his caviare. John had described him as suffering from a number of disabilities, his health was not good and he was ashamed of the disreputable fact that his father was an M.P. Another friend wrote perceptively that Firbank 'was really too fastidious ever to be cheap, unless it is cheap to be forever striving not to be so'.

Firbank seems to have been tolerant of the conversation of undergraduates and quite tongue-tied in the presence of women. He had a mother who spoiled him, doted on him and whom he survived by only two years. No doubt his only real happiness lay in his extraordinary work.

*

When he was at Cambridge Firbank spent a great deal of time with Monsignor Barnes, the Catholic chaplain to the University. He had strongly mystical religious feelings, but he told the musician and artist Lord Berners that 'The Church of Rome wouldn't have me and so I mock at her.' For whatever reason, Firbank became the most elegant writer of ecclesiastical comedy since Trollope and, unlike Trollope's, his books have a strong religious sense. They contain the marvellous sayings of the devout, such as the pronouncement by a Mrs Creswell (*Vainglory*) who wrote in *The Red Rose of Martyrdom*, 'If we are all part of God then God must *indeed* be horrible', and the confession of St Laura de Nanzianzi in *The Flower beneath the Foot* that 'Some girls are born organically good. I wasn't . . .' It was the same finally sanctified Mademoiselle de Nanzianzi who always prayed, 'Oh, help me, Heaven, to be decorative and do right.'

Firbank could, if called upon, turn a Wildean epigram. 'I'm sure your play was exquisite; or it would have had a longer run.' But his chief stylistic gambit, and one he managed brilliantly, was the juxtaposition of the ornate and the banal, continually puncturing his most pretentious moments. Take two examples.

In her cooking he found his landlady solicitous enough . . .
In her supremest flights the good woman would seldom get
beyond suet. And even this was in her most Debussyish vein.
(*Vainglory*)

'In any other age, of course, he would have ambled along in
the retinue of some great lady . . .'
'Oh, be thankful,' Mrs Barrow began. 'As it is, with a little
influence, he's hoping to get into some garage.'
'Poor young man,' Mrs Shamefoot said, with sympathy.
'Such a bending life!' (*Vainglory*)

How can you introduce the newcomer to Firbank's world; what
are the books all about? They are about characters who, in the
tradition of Congreve and Dickens, Wodehouse and Beachcomber,
have the most outrageous names – Mrs Shamefoot, Doctor Pantry,
Lady Parrula de Panzoust, Mrs Thoroughfare, Dr Cunliffe Babcock,
Miss Miami Mouth, Father Felicitas, Winsome Brookes and Mr
Calvally. They are about people who want to get themselves into
stained-glass windows, have their dogs Christened or merely live in
the sunlight and long to move to the legendary city of Cuna, 'City of
Mimosa, Cuna, City of Arches, Queen of the Tropics, Paradise – and
enter society'.

Firbank's novels are about all these things, but chiefly they are
about the creation of a new sort of fiction, apparently as effortless as
scattering fragments of dialogue which leave everything to the
imagination. In fact it is minutely calculated, perfectly timed and
leaves absolutely nothing to chance.

*

In June 1921, living for the summer in a house in the rue de
Reservoirs in Versailles, Firbank began *The Flower beneath the
Foot*, the book which took him longest to write and on which he
lavished especial care. He scrawled it, as he always did, in huge
handwriting on enormous postcards. He created the Kingdom of
Pisuerga with its Royal Family, her Dreaminess the Queen, His
Weariness the Prince Yousef and King Willie who 'had the air of a

tired pastry cook'. He also conjured up that troubled soul the future St Laura de Nanzianzi, who owed her speed at reading to constant practice 'on the screens at cinemas'. There is also a Countess Medusa Rapper, whose favourite Shakespeare play is a work she believes to be called 'Julia Sees Her'.

As usual in a Firbank novel the plot is of no particular importance. The characters glide by, perturbed by unfounded rumours of fleas found in the Ritz, tormented by love, noticing with relief, 'How one's face unbends in gardens,' or slipping sadly into the eventful life of a religious order. As usual the moment, and not the sequence of events, is all important.

> 'A marriage like our's dear, was so utterly unworth-while . . .'
> 'I'm not sure, dear, that I comprehend altogether?'
> 'Seagulls' wings as they fan one's face . . .'
> 'It's vile and wrong to shoot them: but oh! how I wish your happiness depended, ever so little, on me.'
> The Countess averted her eyes. Waterfowl, like sadness passing, hovered and soared overhead, casting their dark fleeting shadows to the white, drowned clouds, in the receptive waters of the lake.
> 'I begin to wish I'd brought grapes,' she breathed.
> 'Heavy stodgy pears. So do I!'

The book also has some of his best and most economical comic passages, with dialogue which might also have occurred to the creator of Jeeves.

> 'Whenever I go out,' the King complained, 'I get an impression of raised hats.'
> It was seldom King William of Pisuerga spoke in the present tense, and Dr Babcock looked perturbed.
> 'Raised hats, sir?' he murmured in impressive tones.
> 'Nude heads, doctor.'

*

By the time he wrote *The Flower beneath the Foot* Firbank had his dedicated admirers. Writers like Aldous Huxley and Osbert Sitwell understood his quality, and his next book, *Prancing Nigger*, actually achieved commercial success in America. In 1926 he wrote his last novel, *Concerning the Eccentricities of Cardinal Pirelli*. This work ends with the rakish cardinal, stripped of everything but his mitre, pursuing an altar boy, known variously as 'Chicklet', 'Don Wilful' and 'Don April Showers', about his cathedral. The image is absurd and powerful, either of an old man chasing love or of a writer in desperate pursuit of an elusive sentence.

In the spring of 1926 Firbank returned, from a journey to Egypt, to Rome, a city where he seems to have had few close friends. He died alone in a room in the Hotel Quirinale. Lord Berners was in Italy and, remembering what Firbank had told him about being rejected by the Catholic Church, had him buried in the Protestant cemetery with Keats and Shelley. Later Berners discovered that Firbank was, in fact, a Catholic, and that his talk of rejection referred to his no doubt misguided wish to become a priest. It was then too late to rectify the mistake, and the novelist remains buried under the Pyramid of Cestius, a spot, Lord Berners pointed out in his description of the event, where some extremely eccentric nightingales sing loudly in the daytime.

The most fitting epitaph for his extraordinary talent would be a quotation from *The Flower beneath the Foot*. In this book a Miss Hopkins confesses that she once met Ronald Firbank and adds, 'He told me writing books was by no means easy.'

THE FLOWER
BENEATH THE FOOT

To
Madame Mathieu
and
Mademoiselle Dora Garnier-Pagès

'Some girls are born organically good: I wasn't.'

St Laura de Nazianzi

'It was about my eighteenth year that I conquered my *Ego*.'

Ibid

I

Neither her Gaudiness the Mistress of the Robes nor her Dreaminess the Queen were feeling quite themselves. In the Palace all was speculation. Would they be able to attend the *Fêtes* in honour of King Jotifa, and Queen Thleeanouhee of the Land of Dates? – Court opinion seemed largely divided. Countess Medusa Rappa, a woman easily disturbable, was prepared to wager what the Countess of Tolga 'liked' (she knew), that another week would find the Court shivering beneath the vaulted domes of the Summer Palace.

'I fear I've no time (or desire) now, Medusa,' the Countess answered, moving towards the Royal apartments, 'for making bets'; though, turning before the ante-room door, she nodded: 'Done!'

She found her sovereign supine on a couch piled with long Tunisian cushions, while a maid of honour sat reading to her aloud:

'*Live with an aim, and let that aim be high!*' the girl was saying as the Countess approached.

'Is that you, Violet?' her Dreaminess inquired without looking round.

'How is your condition, Madam?' the Countess anxiously murmured.

'Tell me, do, of a place that soothes and lulls one . . .'

The Countess of Tolga considered.

'Paris,' she hazarded.

'Ah! Impossible.'

'The Summer Palace, then,' the Countess ejaculated, examining her long slender fingers that were like the tendrils of a plant.

'Dr Cuncliffe Babcock flatly forbids it,' the Royal woman declared, starting slightly at the sound of a gun. 'That must be *the Dates!*' she said. And in effect, a vague reverberation, as of individual cheering, resounded fitfully from afar. 'Give me my diamond

anemones,' the Queen commanded, and motioning to her Maid:
'Pray conclude, mademoiselle, those lofty lines.'

With a slight sigh, the lectress took up the posture of a Dying
Intellectual.

'*Live with an aim, and let that aim be high!*' she reiterated in
tones tinged perceptibly with emotion.

'But not *too* high, remember, Mademoiselle de Nazianzi . . .'

There was a short pause. And then –

'Ah, Madam! What a dearest he is!'

'I think you forget yourself,' the Queen murmured with a
quelling glance. 'You had better withdraw.'

'He has such strength! One could niche an idol in his dear, dinted
chin.'

'Enough!'

And a moment later the enflamed girl left the room warbling
softly: *Depuis le Jour.*

'Holy Virgin,' the Countess said, addressing herself to the
ceiling. 'Should his Weariness, the Prince, yield himself to this
caprice . . .'

The Queen shifted a diamond bangle from one of her arms to the
other.

'She reads at such a pace,' she complained, 'and when I asked her
where she had learnt to read so quickly she replied "On the screens
at Cinemas."'

'I do not consider her at all distinguished,' the Countess commented, turning her eyes away towards the room.

It was a carved-ceiled and rather lofty room, connected by tall
glass doors with other rooms beyond. Peering into one of these the
Countess could see reflected the 'throne', and a little piece of broken
Chippendale brought from England, that served as a stand for a
telephone, wrought in ormolu and rock-crystal, which the sun's
rays at present were causing to emit a thousand playful sparks.
Tapestry panels depicting the Loves of *Mejnoun and Leileh* half
concealed the silver *boiseries* of the walls, while far down the room,
across old rugs from Chirvan that were a marvellous wonder,
showed fortuitous jardinières filled with every kind of flowering

plant. Between the windows were canopied recesses, denuded of their statues by the Queen's desire, 'in order that they might appear suggestive', while through the windows themselves the Countess could catch, across the forecourt of the castle, a panorama of the town below, with the State Theatre and the Garrisons, and the Houses of Parliament, and the Hospital, and the low white dome, crowned by turquoise-tinted tiles, of the Cathedral, which was known to all churchgoers as *the Blue Jesus*.

'It would be a fatal connexion,' the Queen continued, 'and it must never, never be!'

By way of response the Countess exchanged with her sovereign a glance that was known in Court circles as her *tortured-animal* look. 'Their Oriental majesties,' she observed, 'to judge from the din, appear to have already endeared themselves with the mob!'

The Queen stirred slightly amid her cushions.

'For the aggrandisement of the country's trade, an alliance with Dateland is by no means to be depreciated,' she replied, closing her eyes as though in some way or other this bullion to the State would allow her to gratify her own wildest whims, the dearest, perhaps, of which was to form a party to excavate (for objects of art) among the ruins of Chedorlahomor, a *faubourg* of Sodom.

'Am I right, Madam, in assuming it's Bananas? . . .' the Countess queried.

But at that moment the door opened, and his Weariness the Prince entered the room in all his tinted Orders.

Handsome to tears, his face, even when he had been a child, lacked innocence. His was of that *magnolia* order of colouring, set off by pleasantly untamed eyes, and teeth like flawless pearls.

'You've seen them? What are they like . . . ? Tell Mother, darling?' the Queen exclaimed.

'They're merely dreadful,' his Weariness, who had been to the railway-station to welcome the Royal travellers, murmured in a voice extinct with boredom.

'They're in European dress, dear?' his mother questioned.

'The King had on a frock coat and a cap . . .'

'And she?'

'A tartan skirt, and checked wool stockings.'

'She has great individuality, so I hear, marm,' the Countess ventured.

'Individuality be –! No one can doubt she's a terrible woman.' The Queen gently groaned.

'I see life today,' she declared, 'in the colour of mould.'

The Prince protruded a shade the purple violet of his tongue.

'Well, its depressing,' he said, 'for us all, with the Castle full of blacks.'

'That is the least of my worries,' the Queen observed. 'Oh, Yousef, Yousef,' she added, 'do you wish to break my heart?'

The young man protruded some few degrees further his tongue.

'I gather you're alluding to Laura!' he remarked.

'But what can you *see* in her?' his mother mourned.

'She suits my feelings,' the Prince simply said.

'Peuh!'

'She meets my needs.'

'She's so housemaid . . . I hardly know . . . !' The Queen raised beautiful hands, bewildered.

'Très gutter, ma'am,' the Countess murmured, dropping her voice to a half-whisper.

'She saves us from *cliché*,' the Prince indignantly said.

'She saves us from nothing,' his mother returned. 'Oh, Yousef, Yousef. And what *cerné* eyes, my son. I suppose you were gambling all night at the Château des Fleurs?'

'Just hark to the crowds!' the Prince evasively said. And never too weary to receive an ovation, he skipped across the room towards the nearest window, where he began blowing kisses to the throng.

'Give them the Smile Extending, darling,' his mother beseeched.

'Won't you rise and place your arm about him, Madam?' the Countess suggested.

'I'm not feeling at all up to the mark,' her Dreaminess demurred, passing her fingers over her hair.

'There is sunshine, ma'am . . . and you have your *anemones* on . . .' the Countess cajoled, 'and to please the people, you ought indeed to squeeze him.' And she was begging and persuading the

Queen to rise as the King entered the room preceded by a shapely page (of sixteen) with cheeks fresher than milk.

'Go to the window, Willie,' the Queen exhorted her Consort, fixing an eye on the last trouser button that adorned his long, straggling legs.

The King, who had the air of a tired pastry-cook, sat down.

'We feel,' he said, 'today, we've had our fill of stares!'

'One little bow, Willie,' the Queen entreated, 'that wouldn't kill you.'

'We'd give perfect worlds,' the King went on, 'to go, by Ourselves, to bed.'

'Get rid of the noise for me. *Quiet them.* Or I'll be too ill,' the Queen declared, 'to leave my room tonight!'

'Should I summon Whisky, Marm?' the Countess asked, but before there was time to reply the Court physician, Dr Cuncliffe Babcock, was announced.

'I feel I've had a relapse, doctor,' her Dreaminess declared.

Dr Babcock beamed: he had one blind eye – though this did not prevent him at all from seeing all that was going on with the other.

'Leave it to me, Madam,' he assured, 'and I shall pick you up in *no* time!'

'Not Johnnie, doctor?' the Queen murmured with a grimace. For a glass of *Johnnie Walker* at bedtime was the great doctor's favourite receipt.

'No; something a little stronger, I think.'

'We need expert attention, too,' the King intervened.

'You certainly are somewhat pale, sir.'

'Whenever I go out,' the King complained, 'I get an impression of raised hats.'

It was seldom King William of Pisuerga spoke in the singular tense, and Doctor Babcock looked perturbed.

'Raised hats, sir?' he murmured in impressive tones.

'Nude heads, doctor.'

The Queen commenced to fidget. She disliked that the King should appear more interesting than herself.

'These earrings tire me,' she said, 'take them out.'

But the Prince, who seemed to be thoroughly enjoying the success of his appearance with the crowd, had already begun tossing the contents of the flower vases into the street.

'Willie . . . prevent him! Yousef . . . I forbid you!' her Dreaminess faintly shrieked. And to stay her son's despoiling hand she skimmed towards him, when the populace, catching sight of her, redoubled their cheers.

Meanwhile Mademoiselle de Nazianzi had regained her composure. As a niece of her Gaudiness the Mistress of the Robes (the Duchess of Cavaljos), she had made her recent début at Court under the brightest conceivable of conditions.

Laura Lita Carmen Étoile de Nazianzi was more piquant perhaps than pretty. A dozen tiny moles were scattered about her face, while on either side of her delicate nose a large grey eye surveyed the world with a pensive critical glance.

'Scenes like that make one sob with laughter,' she reflected, turning into the corridor where two of the Maids of Honour, like strutting idols, were passing up and down.

'Is she really very ill? Is she *really* dying?' they breathlessly inquired.

Mademoiselle de Nazianzi disengaged herself from their solicitously entwining arms.

'She is not!' she answered, in a voice full of eloquent inflections.

But beguiled by the sound of marching feet, one of the girls had darted forward towards a window.

'Oh, Blanche, Blanche, Blanchie love!' she exclaimed, 'I could dance to the click of your brother's spurs.'

'You'd not be the first to, dear darling!' Mademoiselle de Lambèse replied, adjusting her short shock of hair before a glass.

Mademoiselle de Lambèse believed herself to be a very valuable piece of goods, and seemed to think she had only to smile to stir up an ocean of passion.

'Poor Ann-Jules,' she said: 'I fear he's in the clutches of that awful woman.'

'Kalpurnia?'

'Every night he's at the Opera.'

'I hear she wears the costume of a shoeblack in the new ballet,' Mademoiselle de Nazianzi said, 'and is too strangely extraordinary!'

'Have you decided, Rara,* yet, what you'll wear for the ball?'

'A black gown and three blue flowers on my tummy.'

'After a shrimp-tea with the Archduchess, I feel I *want* no dinner,' Mademoiselle Olga Blumenghast, a girl with slightly hunched shoulders, said, returning from the window.

'Oh? Had she a party?'

'A curé or two, and the Countess Yvorra.'

'Her black-bordered envelopes make one shiver!'

'I thought I should have died it was so dull,' Mademoiselle Olga Blumenghast averred, standing aside to allow his Naughtiness Prince Olaf (a little boy racked by all the troubles of spring) and Mrs Montgomery, the Royal Governess, to pass. They had been out evidently among the crowd, and both were laughing heartily at the asides they had overheard.

''Ow can you be so frivolous, your royal 'ighness?' Mrs Montgomery was expostulating: 'for shame, wicked boy! For shame!' And her cheery British laugh echoed gaily down the corridors.

'Well, *I* took tea at the Ritz,' Mademoiselle de Lambèse related.

'Anybody?'

'Quite a few!'

'There's a rumour that Prince Yousef is entertaining there tonight.'

Mademoiselle Blumenghast tittered.

'Did you hear what he called the lanterns for the *Fête?*' she asked.

'No.'

'A lot of "bloody bladders"!'

'What, what a dearest!' Mademoiselle de Nazianzi sighed beneath her breath. And all along the almost countless corridors as far as her bedroom door she repeated again and again: 'What, *what* a dearest!'

---

* The name by which the future saint was sometimes called among her friends.

II

Beneath a wide golden ceiling people were dancing. A capricious concert waltz, drowsy, intricate, caressing, reached fitfully the supper-room, where a few privileged guests were already assembled to meet King Jotifa and Queen Thleeanouhee of the Land of Dates.

It was one of the regulations of the Court that those commanded to the King's board should assemble some few minutes earlier than the Sovereigns themselves, and the guests at present were mostly leaning stiffly upon their chair-backs, staring vacuously at the olives and salted almonds upon the table-cloth before them. Several of the ladies indeed had taken the liberty to seat themselves, and were beguiling the time by studying the menu or disarranging the smilax, while one dame went as far as to take, and even to nibble, a salted almond. A conversation of a non-private kind (carried on between the thin, authoritative legs of a Court Chamberlain) by Countess Medusa Rappa and the English Ambassadress was being listened to by some with mingled signs of interest.

'Ah! How clever Shakespere!' the Countess was saying. 'How gorgeous! How glowing! I once knew a speech from "Julia Sees Her! . . ." perhaps his greatest *œuvre* of all. Yes! "Julia *Sees* Her" is what I like best of that great, great master.'

The English Ambassadress plied her fan.

'Friends, Comrades, Countrymen,' she murmured, 'I used to know it myself!'

But the lady nibbling almonds was exciting a certain amount of comment. This was the Duchess of Varna, voted by many to be one of the handsomest women of the Court. Living in economical obscurity nearly half the year round, her appearances at the palace were becoming more and more infrequent.

'I knew the Varnas were very hard up, but I did not know they were *starving*,' the Countess Yvorra, a woman with a would-be indulgent face that was something less hard than rock, remarked to her neighbour the Count of Tolga, and dropping her glance from the Count's weak chin she threw a fleeting smile towards his wife, who was looking 'Eastern' swathed in the skin of a blue panther.

'Yes, their affairs it seems are almost desperate,' the Count returned, directing his gaze towards the Duchess.

Well-favoured beyond measure she certainly was, with her immense placid eyes, and bundles of loose, blonde hair. She had a gown the green of Nile Water, that enhanced to perfection the swan-like fairness of her throat and arms.

'I'm thinking of building myself a Villa in the Land of Dates!' she was confiding to the British Ambassador, who was standing beside her on her right. 'Ah, yes! I shall end my days in a country strewn with flowers.'

'You would find it I should say too hot, Duchess.'

'My soul has need of the sun, Sir Somebody!' the Duchess replied, opening with equanimity a great black ostrich fan, and smiling up at him through the sticks.

Sir Somebody Something was a person whose nationality was written all over him. Nevertheless he had, despite a bluff and somewhat rugged manner, a certain degree of feminine sensitiveness, and any reference to the *soul* at all (outside the Embassy Chapel) invariably made him fidget.

'In moderation, Duchess,' he murmured, fixing his eyes upon the golden head of a champagne bottle.

'They say it is a land of love!' the Duchess related, raising indolently an almond to her sinuously chiselled lips.

'And even, so it's said, too,' his Excellency returned, 'of licence!' when just at this turn of things the Royal cortège entered the supper-room to the exhilarating strains of King Goahead's War-March.

Those who had witnessed the arrival of King Jotifa and his Queen earlier in the afternoon were amazed at the alteration of their aspect now. Both had discarded their European attire for the loosely-flowing vestments of their native land, and for a brief while there was some slight confusion among those present as to which was the

25

gentleman and which the lady of the two. The King's beard, long and blonde, should have determined the matter outright, but on the other hand the Queen's necklet of reeds and plumes was so very misleading . . . Nobody in Pisuerga had seen anything to compare with it before. 'Marvellous, though terrifying,' the Court passed verdict.

Attended by their various suites, the Royal party gained their places amid the usual manifestation of loyal respect.

But one of the Royal ladies, as it soon became evident, was not yet come.

'Where's Lizzie, Lois?' King William asked, riveting the Archduchess's empty chair.

'We'd better begin without her, Willie,' the Queen exclaimed, 'you know she never minds.'

And hardly had the company seated themselves when, dogged by a lady-in-waiting and a maid-of-honour, the Archduchess Elizabeth of Pisuerga rustled in.

Very old and very bent, and (even) very beautiful, she was looking, as the grammar-books say, 'meet' to be robbed, beneath a formidable tiara, and wearing a dozen long strands of pearls.

'Forgive me, Willie,' she murmured, with a little high, shrill, tinkling laugh: 'but it was so fine that, after tea, I and a Lady went paddling in the Basin of the Nymphs.'

'How was the water?' the King inquired.

The Archduchess repressed a sneeze. 'Fresh,' she replied, 'but not too . . .'

'After sunset beware, dear Aunt, of chills.'

'But for a frog I believe nothing would have got me out!' the august lady confessed as she fluttered bird-like to her chair.

Forbidden in youth by parents and tutors alike the joys of paddling under pain of chastisement, the Archduchess Elizabeth appeared to find a zest in doing so now. Attended by a chosen lady-in-waiting (as a rule the dowager Marchioness of Lallah Miranda), she liked to slip off to one of the numerous basins or natural grottos in the castle gardens, where she would pass whole hours in wading blissfully about. Whilst paddling, it was her wont to run over those refrains from the vaudevilles and operas (with their many shakes and rippling *cadenzi*) in favour in her day, interspersed at intervals by such cries as: 'Pull up your skirt, Marquise, it's dragging a little, my friend, below the knees . . .' or, 'A shark, a shark!' which was her way of designating anything that had fins, from a carp to a minnow.

'I fear our Archduchess has contracted a slight catarrh,' the Mistress of the Robes, a woman like a sleepy cow, observed, addressing herself to the Duke of Varna upon her left.

'Unless she is more careful, she'll go paddling once too often,' the Duke replied, contemplating with interest, above the moonlight-coloured daffodils upon the table board, one of the button-nosed belles of Queen Thleeanouhee's suite. The young creature, referred to cryptically among the subordinates of the castle as 'Tropical Molly', was finding fault already it seemed, with the food.

'Take it away,' she was protesting in animated tones: 'I'd as soon touch a foot-squashed mango!'

'No *mayonnaise*, miss?' a court-official asked, dropping his face prevailingly to within an inch of her own.

'Take it right away . . . And if you should *dare*, sir, to come any closer . . . !'

The Mistress of the Robes fingered nervously the various Orders of Merit on her sumptuous bosom.

'I trust there will be no contretemps,' she murmured, glancing uneasily towards the Queen of the Land of Dates, who seemed to be lost in admiration of the Royal dinner-service of scarlet plates, that looked like pools of blood upon the cloth.

'What pleases me in your land,' she was expansively telling her host, 'is less your food than the china you serve it on; for with us you know there's none. And now,' she added, marvellously wafting a fork, 'I'm for ever spoilt for shells.'

King William was incredulous.

'With you no china?' he gasped.

'None, sir, none!'

'I could not be more astonished,' the King declared, 'if you told me there were fleas at the Ritz,' a part of which assertion Lady

Something, who was blandly listening, imperfectly chanced to hear.

'Who could credit it!' she breathed, turning to an attaché, a young man all white and penseroso, at her elbow.

'Credit what?'

'Did you not hear what the dear King said?'

'No.'

'It's almost *too* appalling . . .' Lady Something replied, passing a small, nerveless hand across her brow.

'Won't you tell me though?' the young man murmured gently, with his nose in his plate.

Lady Something raised a glass of frozen lemonade to her lips.

'Fleas,' she murmured, 'have been found at the Ritz.'

'. . . . . . ! . . . . ? . . . ! !'

'Oh and *poor* Lady Bertha! And poor good old Mrs Hunter!' And Lady Something looked away in the direction of Sir Somebody, as though anxious to catch his eye.

But the British Ambassador and the Duchess of Varna were weighing the chances of a Grant being allowed by Parliament for the excavation of Chedorlahomor.

'Dear little Chedor,' the Duchess kept on saying, 'I'm sure one would find the most enthralling things there. Aren't *you*, Sir Somebody?'

And they were still absorbed in their colloquy when the King gave the signal to rise.

Although King William had bidden several distinguished Divas from the Opera House to give an account of themselves for the entertainment of his guests, both King Jotifa and Queen Thleeanouhee with disarming candour declared that, to their ears, the music of the West was hardly to be borne.

'Well, I'm not very fond of it either,' her Dreaminess admitted, surrendering her skirts to a couple of rosy boys, and leading the way with airy grace towards an adjacent salon, 'although,' she wistfully added across her shoulder to a high dignitary of the Church, 'I'm trying, it's true, to coax the dear Archbishop to give the first act of

La Tosca in the Blue Jesus . . . Such a perfect setting, and with Desiré Erlinger and Maggie Mellon . . . !'

And as the Court now pressed after her the rules of etiquette became considerably relaxed. Mingling freely with his guests, King William had a hand-squeeze and a fleeting word for each.

'In England,' he paused to inquire of Lady Something, who was warning a dowager, with impressive earnestness, against the Ritz, 'have you ever seen two cooks in a kitchen-garden?'

'No, never, sir!' Lady Something simpered.

'Neither,' the King replied, moving on, 'have *we*.'

The Ambassadress beamed.

'My dear,' she told Sir Somebody, a moment afterwards, 'my dear, the King was simply charming. Really I may say he was more than gracious! He asked me if I had ever seen two cooks in a kitchen-garden, and I said no, never! And he said that neither, either, had he! And oh isn't it so strange how few of us ever have?'

But in the salon one of Queen Thleeanouhee's ladies had been desired by her Dreaminess to sing.

'It seems so long,' she declared, 'since I heard an Eastern voice, and it would be such a relief.'

'By all means,' Queen Thleeanouhee said, 'and let a *darbouka* or two be brought! For what charms the heart more, what touches it more,' she asked, considering meditatively her babouched feet, 'than a *darbouka*?'

It was told that, in the past, her life had been a gallant one, although her adventures, it was believed, had been mostly with men. Those, however, who had observed her conduct closely had not failed to remark how often her eyes had been attracted in the course of the evening towards the dimpled cheeks of the British Ambassadress.

Perceiving her ample form not far away, Queen Thleeanouhee signalled to her amiably to approach.

Née Rosa Bark (and a daughter of the Poet) Lady Something was perhaps not sufficiently tactful to meet all the difficulties of the rôle in which it had pleased life to call her. But still, she tried, and did do her best, which often went far to retrieve her lack of *savoir faire*.

'Life is like that, dear,' she would sometimes say to Sir Somebody, but she would never say what it was that life was like; 'That,' it seemed . . .

'I was just looking for my daughter,' she declared.

'And is she as sympathetic,' Queen Thleeanouhee softly asked, 'as her mamma?'

'She's shy – of the Violet persuasion, but that's not a bad thing in a young girl.'

'Where I reign shyness is a quality which is entirely unknown . . . !'

'It must be astonishing, ma'am,' Lady Something replied, caressing a parure of false jewels, intended, indeed, to deceive no one, 'to be a Queen of a sun-steeped country like yours.'

Queen Thleeanouhee fetched a sigh.

'Dateland – my dear, it's a scorch!' she averred.

'I conclude, ma'am, it's what we should call "conservatory" scenery?' Lady Something murmured.

'It is the land of the jessamine-flower, the little amorous jessamine-flower,' the Queen gently cooed, with a sidelong smiling glance, 'that twines itself sometimes to the right hand, at others to the left, just according to its caprices!'

'It sounds, I fear, to be unhealthy, ma'am.'

'And it is the land also, of romance, my dear, where shyness is a quality which is entirely unknown,' the Queen broke off, as one of her ladies, bearing a darbouka, advanced with an air of purposefulness towards her.

The hum of voices which filled the room might well have tended to dismay a vocalist of modest powers, but the young matron known to the Court as 'tropical Molly', and whom her mistress addressed as Timzra, soon showed herself to be equal to the occasion.

> 'Under the blue gum-tree
> I am sitting waiting,
> Under the blue gum-tree
> I am waiting all alone!'

Her voice reached the ears of the fresh-faced ensigns and the beardless subalterns in the Guard Room far beyond, and startled the pages in the distant dormitories, as they lay smoking on their beds.

And then, the theme changing, and with an ever-increasing passion, fervour and force:

> 'I heard a watch-dog in the night . . .
> Wailing, wailing . . .
> Why is the watch-dog wailing?
> He is wailing for the Moon!'

'That is one of the very saddest songs,' the King remarked, 'that I have ever heard. "Why is the watch-dog wailing? He is wailing for the Moon!"' And the ambitions and mortifications of kingship for a moment weighed visibly upon him.

'Something merrier, Timzra!' Queen Thleeanouhee said.

And throwing back her long love-lilac sleeves, Timzra sang:

> 'A negress with a margaret once lolled frousting in the sun
> Thinking of all the little things that she had left undone . . .
> With a hey, hey, hey, hey, hi, hey ho!'

'She has the air of a cannibal!' the Archduchess murmured behind her fan to his Weariness, who had scarcely opened his lips except to yawn throughout the whole of the evening.

'She has the air of a –' he replied laconically, turning away.

Since the conversation with his mother earlier in the day his thoughts had revolved incessantly around Laura. What had they been saying to the poor wee witch, and whereabouts was she to be found?

Leaving the salon, in the wake of a pair of venerable politicians, who were helping each other along with little touches and pats, he made his way towards the ball-room, where a new dance known as the Pisgah Pas was causing some excitement, and gaining a post of vantage, it was not long before he caught a glimpse of the agile, boyish figure of his betrothed. She passed him, without apparently noticing he was there, in a whirlwind of black tulle, her little hand pressed to the breast of a man like a sulky eagle; and he could not help rejoicing inwardly that, *once* his wife, it would no longer be possible for her to enjoy herself exactly with whom she pleased. As she swept by again he succeeded in capturing her attention, and, nodding meaningly towards a deserted picture-gallery, wandered away towards it. It was but seldom he set foot there, and he amused himself by examining some of the pictures to be seen upon the walls. An old shrew with a rose . . . a drawing of a man alone in the last extremes . . . a pink-robed Christ . . . a seascape, painted probably in winter, with cold, hard colouring . . .

'Yousef?'

'Rara!'

'Let us go outside, dear.'

A night so absolutely soft and calm was delicious after the glare and noise within.

'With whom,' he asked, 'sweetheart, were you last dancing?'

'Only the brother of one of the Queen's Maids, dear,' Mademoiselle de Nazianzi replied. 'After dinner, though,' she tittered, 'when he gets Arabian-Nighty, it's apt to annoy one a scrap!'

'*Arabian-Nighty?*'

'Oh, never mind!'

'But (pardon me, dear) I do.'

'Don't be tiresome, Yousef! The night is too fine,' she murmured, glancing absently away towards the hardly moving trees, from whose branches a thousand drooping necklets of silver lamps palely burned.

Were *those* the 'bladders' then?

Strolling on down hoops of white wistaria in the moon they came to the pillared circle of a rustic temple, commanding a prospect on the town.

'There,' she murmured, smiling elfishly and designating something, far below them, through the moon mist, with her fan, 'is the column of Justice and,' she laughed a little, 'of *Liberty!*'

'And there,' he pointed inconsequently, 'is *the Automobile Club!*'

'And beyond it . . . the Convent of the Flaming-Hood . . .'

'And those blue revolving lights; can you see them, Rara?'

'Yes, dear . . . what are *they*, Yousef?'

'Those,' he told her, contemplating her beautiful white face against the dusky bloom, 'are the lights of the Café Cleopatra!'

'And what,' she questioned, as they sauntered on, pursued by all the sweet perfumes of the night, 'are those berried-shrubs that smell so passionately?'

'I don't know,' he said. 'Kiss me, Rara!'

'No, no.'

'Why not?'

'Not now!'

'Put your arm about me, dear.'

'What a boy he is!' she murmured, gazing up into the starry clearness.

Overhead a full moon, a moon of circumstance, rode high in the sky, defining phantasmally, far off, the violet-farded hills beyond the town.

'To be out there among the silver bean-fields!' he said.

'Yes, Yousef,' she sighed, starting at a Triton's face among the trailing ivy on the castle wall. Beneath it, half concealed by water-flags, lay a miniature lake: as a rule, nobody now went near the lake at all, since the Queen had called it '*appallingly smelly*', so that for rendezvous it was quite ideal.

'Tell me, Yousef,' she presently said, pausing to admire the beautiful shadow of an orange-tree on the path before them: 'tell me, dear, when Life goes like that to one – what does one do!!'

He shrugged. 'Usually nothing,' he replied, the tip of his tongue (like the point of a blade) peeping out between his teeth.

'Ah, but isn't that being strong?' she said half audibly, fixing her eyes as though fascinated upon his lips.

'Why,' he demanded, with an engaging smile that brought half-moons to his hollow cheeks, 'what has the world been doing to Rara?'

'At this instant, Yousef,' she declared, 'it brings her nothing but Joy!'

'You're happy, my sweet, with me?'

'No one knows, dearest, how much I love you.'

'Kiss me, Rara,' he said again.

'Bend, then,' she answered, as the four quarters of the twelve strokes of midnight rang out leisurely from the castle clock.

'I've to go to the Ritz!' he announced.

'And I should be going in.'

Retracing reluctantly their steps they were soon in earshot of the ball, and their close farewells were made accompanied by selections from The Blue Banana.

She remained a few moments gazing as though entranced at his retreating figure, and would have, perhaps, run after him with some little capricious message, when she became aware of someone watching her from beneath the shadow of a garden vase.

Advancing steadily and with an air of nonchalance, she recognized the delicate, sexless silhouette and slightly hunched shoulders of Olga Blumenghast, whose exotic attraction had aroused not a few heart-burnings (and even feuds) among several of the grandes dames about the court.

Poised flatly against the vase's sculptured plinth, she would have scarcely been discernible but for the silver glitter of her gown.

'Olga? Are you faint?'

'No; only my slippers are torture.'

'I'd advise you to change them, then!'

'It's not altogether my feet, dear, that ache . . .'

'Ah, I see,' Mademoiselle de Nazianzi said, stooping enough to scan the stormy, soul-tossed eyes of her friend: 'you're suffering, I suppose on account of Ann-Jules?'

'He's such a gold-fish, Rara . . . any fingers that will throw him bread . . .'

'And there's no doubt, I'm afraid, that lots do!' Mademoiselle de Nazianzi answered lucidly, sinking down by her side.

'I would give all my soul to him, Rara . . . my chances of heaven!'

'Your chances, Olga –' Mademoiselle de Nazianzi murmured, avoiding some bird-droppings with her skirt.

'How I envy the men, Rara, in his platoon!'

'Take away his uniform, Olga, and what does he become?'

'Ah what – !'

'No . . . Believe me, my dear, he's not worth the trouble!'

Mademoiselle Blumenghast clasped her hands brilliantly across the nape of her neck.

'I want to possess him at dawn, at dawn,' she broke out: 'Beneath a sky striped with green . . .'

'Oh, Olga!'

'And I never shall rest,' she declared, turning away on a languid heel, 'until I *do*.'

Meditating upon the fever of Love, Mademoiselle de Nazianzi directed her course slowly towards her room. She lodged in that part of the palace known as 'The Bachelors' Wing', where she had a delicious little suite just below the roof.

'If she loved him absolutely,' she told herself, as she turned the handle of her door, 'she would not care about the colour of the sky; even if it snowed or hailed!'

Depositing her fan upon the lid of an old wedding-chest that formed a couch, she smiled contentedly about her. It would be a wrench abandoning this little apartment that she had identified already with herself, when the day should come to leave it for others more spacious in the Keep. Although scarcely the size of a ship's cabin, it was amazing how many people one could receive together at a time merely by pushing the piano back against the wall and wheeling the wedding-chest on to the stairs; and once no fewer than seventeen persons had sat down to a birthday *fête* without being made too much to feel like herrings. In the so-called salon, divided from her bedroom by a folding lacquer screen, hung a few studies in oils executed by herself, which, except to the initiated, or the naturally instinctive, looked sufficiently enigmatic against a wall-paper with a stealthy design.

Yes, it would be a wrench to quit the little place, she reflected, as she began setting about her toilet for the night. It was agreeable going to bed late without anybody's aid, when one could pirouette interestingly before the mirror in the last stages of déshabillé, and do a thousand (and one) things besides* that one might otherwise

---

* Always a humiliating recollection with her in after years. *Vide* 'Confessions'.

lack the courage for. But this evening, being in no frivolous mood, she changed her ball dress swiftly for a robe-de-chambre bordered deeply with ermines, that made her feel nearer somehow to Yousef, and helped her to realize her position in its various facets as future Queen.

'Queen!' she breathed, trailing her fur flounces towards the window.

Already the blue revolving lights of the Café Cleopatra were growing paler with the dawn, and the moon had veered a little towards the Convent of the Flaming-Hood. Ah . . . how often as a lay boarder there had she gazed up towards the palace wondering half-shrinkingly what life 'in the world' was like; for there had been a period, indeed, when the impulse to take the veil had been strong with her – more, perhaps, to be near one of the nuns whom she had *idolized* than from any more immediate vocation.

She remained immersed in thoughts, her introspectiveness fanned insensibly by the floating zephyrs that spring with morning. The slight sway-sway of the trees, the awakening birds in the castle eaves, the green-veined bougainvillaeas that fringed her sill – these thrilled her heart with joy. All virginal in the early dawn what magic the world possessed! Slow speeding clouds like knots of pink roses came blowing across the sky, sailing away in titanic bouquets above the town.

Just such a morning should be their wedding-day! she mused, beginning lightly to apply the contents of a jar of milk of almonds to her breast and arms. Ah, before that Spina Christi lost its leaves, or that swallow should migrate . . . that historic day would come!

Troops . . . hysteria . . . throngs . . . The Blue Jesus packed to suffocation . . . She could envisage it all.

And there would be a whole holiday in the Convent, she reflected, falling drowsily at her bedside to her knees.

'Oh! help me, heaven,' she prayed, 'to be decorative and to do right! Let me always look young, never more then sixteen or seventeen – at the *very* outside, and let Yousef love me – as much as I do him. And I thank you for creating such a darling, God (for he's a perfect dear), and I can't tell you how much I love him; especially when he wags it! I mean his tongue . . . Bless all the sisters at the Flaming-Hood – above all Sister Ursula . . . and be sweet, besides, to old Jane . . . Show me the straight path! And keep me ever free from the malicious scandal of the Court. Amen.'

And her orisons (end in a brief self-examination) over, Mademoiselle de Nazianzi climbed into bed.

III

In the Salle de Prince or Cabinet d'Antoine, above the Café Cleopatra, Madame Wetme, the wife of the proprietor, sat perusing the Court gazettes.

It was not often that a *cabinet particulier* like Antoine was disengaged at luncheon time, being as a rule reserved many days in advance, but it had been a 'funny' season, as the saying went, and there was the possibility that a party of late-risers might look in yet (officers, or artistes from the Halls), who had been passing a night 'on the tiles'. But Madame Wetme trusted not. It was pleasant to escape every now and again from her lugubrious back-drawing-room that only faced a wall, or to peruse the early newspapers without having first to wait for them. And today precisely was the day for the hebdomadal *causerie* in the *Jaw-waws' Journal* on matters appertaining to society, signed by that ever popular diarist 'Eva Schnerb'.

'Never,' Madame Wetme read, 'was a gathering more brilliant than that which I witnessed last night! I stood in a corner of the Great ball-room and literally *gasped* at the wealth of jewels . . . Beauty and bravery abounded, but no one, *I* thought, looked better than our most gracious Queen, etc. . . . . Among the supper-guests I saw their Excellencies Prince and Princess Paul de Pismiche – the Princess impressed me as being *just* a trifle pale: she is by no means strong, and unhappily our nefarious climate does not agree with everybody! – their Excellencies Sir Somebody and Lady Somebody (Miss Ivy Something charming in cornflower *charmeuse* danced indefatigably all the evening, as did also one of the de Lambèse girls); the Count and Countess of Tolga – she all in blue furs and literally *ablaze* with gorgeous gems (I hear on excellent authority she is shortly relinquishing her post of Woman of the Bedchamber which she finds is really too arduous for her); the Duchess of Varna, looking veritably radiant (by the way where has she been?) in the palest of pistachio-green mashlaks, which are all the rage at present.

'*Have you a Mashlak?*'

'Owing to the visit of King Jotifa and Queen Thleeanouhee, the Eastern mashlak is being worn by many of the smart women about the Court. I saw an example at the Opera the other night in silver and gold *lamé* that I thought too –' Madame Wetme broke off to look up, as a waiter entered the room.

'Did Madame ring?'

'No! . . .'

'Then it must have been "Ptolemy"!' the young man murmured, bustling out.

'I dare say. When will you know your bells?' Madame Wetme retorted, returning with a headshake to the gazette: her beloved Eva was full of information this week and breathlessly she read on:

'I saw Minnie, Lady Violetrock (whose daughter Sonia is being educated here), at the garden *fête* the other day at the Château des Fleurs, looking chic as she *always* does, in a combination of petunia and purple ninon raffling a donkey.

'I hear on the best authority that before the Court goes to the Summer Palace later on there will be at least *one* more Drawing-room. Applications, from those entitled to attend, should be made to the Lord Chamberlain as *soon* as possible.'

One more Drawing-room –! The journal fell from Madame Wetme's hand.

'I'm getting on now,' she reflected, 'and if I'm not presented soon I never will be . . .'

She raised imploring eyes to the mural imagery – to the 'Cleopatra couchant', to the 'Arrival of Anthony', to the 'Sphinx', to the 'Temple of Ra', as though seeking inspiration. 'Ah my God!' she groaned.

But Madame Wetme's religion, her cruel God, was the *Chic*: the God Chic.

The sound of music from below reached her faintly. There was not a better orchestra (even at the Palace) than that which discoursed at the Café Cleopatra – and they played, the thought had sometimes pleased her, the same identical tunes!

'Does it say when?' she murmured, re-opening the gazette. No: but it would be 'before the Court left' . . . And when would that be?

'I have good grounds for believing,' she continued to read, 'that in order to meet his creditors the Duke of Varna is selling a large portion of his country estate.'

If it were true . . . Madame Wetme's eyes rested in speculation on the oleanders in the great flower-tubs before the Café; if it were true, why the Varnas must be desperate, and the Duchess ready to do anything. 'Anything – for remuneration,' she murmured rising and going towards a table usually used for correspondence. And seating herself with a look of decision, she opened a leather writing-pad, full of crab-coloured, ink-marked blotting-paper.

In the fan-shaped mirror above the writing-table she could see herself in fancy, all veils and aigrettes, as she would be on 'the day' when coiffed by Ernst.

'Among a bevy of charming débutantes, no one looked more striking than Madame Wetme, who was presented by the Duchess of Varna.' Being a client of the house (with an unpaid bill) she could *dictate* to Eva . . . But first, of course, she must secure the Duchess. And taking up her pen she wrote: 'Madame Wetme would give the Duchess of Varna fifty thousand crowns to introduce her at Court.' A trifle terse perhaps?? Madame Wetme considered. How if the Duchess should take offence . . . It was just conceivable! And besides, by specifying no fixed sum, she might be got for less.

'Something more mysterious, more delicate in style . . .' Madame Wetme murmured with a sigh, beginning the letter anew:

'If the Duchess of Varna will call on Madame Wetme this afternoon, about five, and partake of a cup of tea, she will hear of something *to her advantage*.'

Madame Wetme smiled. 'That should get her!' she reflected, and selecting an envelope, she directed it boldly to the Ritz. 'Being hard up, she is sure to be there!' she reasoned, as she left the room in quest of a page.

The French maid of the Duchess of Varna was just putting on her mistress's shoes, in a private sitting-room at the Ritz, when Madame Wetme's letter arrived.

The pleasure of being in the capital once more, after a long spell of the country, had given her an appetite for her lunch and she was feeling braced after an excellent meal.

'I shall not be back, I expect, till late, Louison,' she said to her maid, 'and should anyone inquire where I am, I shall either be at the Palace, or at the Skating Rink.'

'Madame la Duchesse will not be going to her corsetier's?'

'It depends if there's time. What did I do with my shopping-list?' the Duchess replied, gathering up abstractedly a large, becoroneted vanity-case and a parasol. She had a gown of khaki and daffodil and a black tricorne hat trimmed with green. 'Give me my other sun-shade, the jade – and don't forget – On me trouvera, soit au Palais Royal, soit au Palais de Glace!' she enjoined, sailing quickly out.

Leaving the Ritz by a side door, she found herself in a quiet shady street bordering the Regina Gardens. Above, a sky so blue, so clear, so luminous seemed to cry out: 'Nothing matters! Why worry? Be sanguine! Amuse yourself!! Nothing matters!'

Traversing the gardens, her mind preoccupied by Madame Wetme's note, the Duchess branched off into a busy thoroughfare leading towards the Opera, in whose vicinity lay the city's principal shops. To learn of anything to one's advantage was, of course, always welcome, but there were various other claims upon her besides that afternoon, which she was unable, or loath, to ignore – the palace, a *thé dansant* or two, and then her favourite rink . . . although the unfortunate part was that most of the rink instructors were still unpaid, and on the last occasion she had hired one to waltz with her he had taken advantage of the fact by pressing her waist with greater freedom than she felt he need have done.

Turning into the Opera Square with its fine arcades, she paused, half furtively, before a florist's shop. Only her solicitors and a few in the secret were aware that the premises known as *Haboubet of Egypt* were her own; for, fearful lest they might be occupied one day by sheriffs' officers, she had kept the little business venture the closest mystery. Lilies 'from Karnak', Roses 'from the Land of Punt' (all grown in the gardens of her country house, in the purlieus of the capital) found immediate and daily favour among amateurs of the choice. Indeed, as her gardener frequently said, the demand for Roses from the Land of Punt was more than he could possibly cope with without an extra man.

'I may as well run in and take whatever there's in the till,' she reflected – 'not that, I fear, there's much . . .'

The superintendent, a slim Tunisian boy, was crouching pitcher-posture upon the floor, chanting languidly to himself, his head supported by an osier pannier lately arrived from 'Punt'.

'Up, Bachir!' the Duchess upbraided. 'Remember the fresh consignments perish while you dream there and sing.'

The young Tunisian smiled.

He worshipped the Duchess, and the song he was improvising as she entered had been inspired by her. In it (had she known) he had led her by devious tender stages to his father's fonduk at Tifilalet 'on the blue Lake of Fetzara', where he was about to present her to the Cheik and the whole assembled village as his chosen bride.

The Duchess considered him. He had a beautiful face spoiled by a bad complexion, which doubtless (the period of puberty passed) he would outgrow.

'Consignment him come not two minute,' the youth replied.

'Ah Bachir? Bachir!'

'By the glorious Koran, I will swear it.'

'Be careful not to shake those *Alexandrian Balls*,' the Duchess peremptorily enjoined, pointing towards some Guelder-roses – 'or they'll fall before they're sold!'

'No matter at all. They sold already! An American lady this morning she purchase all my Alexandrian-balls; two heavy bunch.'

'Let me see your takings . . .'

With a smile of triumph, Bachir turned towards the till. He had the welfare of the establishment at heart as well as his own, and of an evening often he would flit, garbed in his long gandourah, through the chief Cafés and Dancings of the city, a vast pannier upon his head heaped high with flowers, which he would dispose of to dazzled clients for an often exorbitant sum. But for these excursions of

his (which ended on occasion in adventure) he had received no
authority at all.

'Not so bad,' the Duchess commented. 'And, as there's to be a
Court again soon, many orders for bouquets are sure to come
in!'

'I call in outside hands to assist me: I summon Ouardi! He an
Armenian boy. Sympathetic. My friend. More attached to him am I
than a branch of jessamine is about a vine.'

'I suppose he's capable?' the Duchess murmured, pinning a
green-ribbed orchid to her dress.

'The garlands of Ouardi would make even a jackal look
bewitching!'

'Ah: he has taste?'

'I engage my friend. Much work always in the month of Redjeb!'

'Engage nobody,' the Duchess answered as she left the shop,
'until I come again.'

Hailing in the square one of the little shuttered cabs of the city,
she directed the driver to drop her at the palace gates, and pursued
by an obstreperous newsboy with an evening paper, yelling 'Chedorlahomor! Sodom! Extra Special!', the cab clattered off at a
languid trot. Under the plane-trees, near the Houses of Parliament,
she was overtaken by the large easy-stepping horses of the Ambassadress of England and acknowledged with a winning movement of
the wrist Lady Something's passing accueil. It was yet not quite the
correct hour for the Promenade, where beneath the great acacias
Society liked best to ride or drive, but, notwithstanding, that zealous
reporter of social deeds, the irrepressible Eva Schnerb, was already
on the prowl and able with satisfaction to note: 'I saw the Duchess of
Varna early driving in the Park, all alone in a little one-horse shay,
that really looked more elegant than any Delaunay-Belleville!'

Arriving before the palace gates, the Duchess perceived an array
of empty carriages waiting in the drive, which made her apprehen-
sive of a function. She had anticipated an intimate chat with the
Queen alone, but this it seemed was not to be.

Following a youthful page with a *resigned* face down a long black
rug woven with green and violet flowers, who left her with a sigh (as

if disappointed of a tip) in charge of a couple of giggling colleagues, who, in turn, propelled her towards a band of sophisticated-looking footmen and grim officials, she was shown at last into a vast white drawing-room whose ceiling formed a dome.

Knowing the Queen's interest in the Chedorlahomor Excavation Bill, a number of representative folk, such as the wives of certain Politicians or Diplomats, as well as a few of her own more immediate circle, had called to felicitate her upon its success. Parliament had declared itself willing to do the unlimited graceful by all those concerned, and this in a great measure was due to the brilliant wire-pulling of the Queen.

She was looking singularly French in a gold helmet and a violet Vortniansky gown, and wore a rope of faultless pearls, clasped very high beneath the chin.

'I hope the Archbishop will bless the excavators' tools!' she was saying to the wife of the Premier as the Duchess entered. 'The *picks* at any rate . . .'

That lady made no reply. In presence of Royalty she would usually sit and smile at her knees, raising her eyes from time to time to throw, beneath her lashes, an ineffable expiring glance.

'God speed them safe home again!' the Archduchess Elizabeth who was busy knitting said. An ardent philanthropist, she had begun already making 'comforts' for the men, as the nights in the East are cold. The most philanthropic perhaps of all the Royal Family, her hobby was designing, for the use of the public, sanitary, but artistic, places of necessity on a novel system of ventilation. The King had consented to open (and it was expected appropriately) one of these in course of construction in the Opera Square.

'Amen,' the Queen answered, signalling amiably to the Duchess of Varna, whose infrequent visits to court disposed her always to make a fuss of her.

But no fuss the Queen could make of the Duchess of Varna could exceed that being made by Queen Thleeanouhee, in a far-off corner, of her Excellency Lady Something. The sympathy, the *entente* indeed that had arisen between these two ladies, was exercising considerably the minds of certain members of the diplomatic corps, although, had anyone wished to eavesdrop, their conversation upon the whole must have been found to be anything but esoteric.

'What I want,' Queen Thleeanouhee was saying, resting her hand confidentially on her Excellency's knee, 'what I want is an English maid with Frenchified fingers – Is there such a thing to be had?'

'But surely –' Lady Something smiled: for the servant-topic was one she felt at home on.

'In Dateland, my dear, servant girls are nothing but sluts.'

'Life is like *that*, ma'am, I regret, indeed, to have to say: I once had a housemaid who had lived with Sarah Bernhardt, and oh, wasn't she a terror!' Lady Something declared, warding off a little black bat-eared dog who was endeavouring to scramble on to her lap.

'Teddywegs, Teddywegs!' the Archduchess exclaimed, jumping up and advancing to capture her pet. 'He arrived from London not later than this morning,' she said; 'from the Princess Elsie of England.'

'He looks like some special litter,' Lady Something remarked.

'How the dear girl loves animals!'

'The rumour of her betrothal it seems is quite without foundation?'

'To my nephew: ah alas . . .'

'Prince Yousef and she are of an equal age!'

'She is interested in Yousef I'm inclined to believe; but the worst of life is, nearly everyone marches to a different tune,' the Archduchess replied.

'One hears of her nothing that isn't agreeable.'

'Like her good mother, Queen Glory,' the Archduchess said, 'one feels, of course, she's all she should be.'

Lady Something sighed.

'Yes . . . and even *more!*' she murmured, letting fall a curtsey to King William who had entered. He had been lunching at the Headquarters of the Girl Guides and wore the uniform of a general.

'What is the acme of nastiness?' he paused of the English Ambassadress to inquire.

Lady Something turned paler than the white candytuft that is found on ruins. 'Oh *la*, sir,' she stammered, 'how should I know!'

The King looked the shrinking matron slowly up and down. 'The supreme disgust –'

'Oh *la*, sir!' Lady Something stammered again.

But the King took pity on her evident confusion. 'Tepid potatoes,' he answered, 'on a stone-cold plate.'

The Ambassadress beamed.

'I trust the warmth of the girls, sir, compensated you for the coldness of the plates?' she ventured.

'The inspection, in the main, was satisfactory! Although I noticed that one or two of the guides seemed inclined to lead astray,' the King replied, regarding Teddywegs, who was inquisitively sniffing his spurs.

'He's strange yet to everything,' the Archduchess commented.

'What's this – a new dog?'

'From Princess Elsie . . .'

'They say she's stupid, but I do not know that intellect is always a blessing!' the King declared, drooping his eyes to his abdomen with an air of pensive modesty.

'Poor child, she writes she is tied to the shore, so that I suppose she is unable to leave dear England.'

'Tied to it?'

'And bound till goodness knows.'

'As was Andromeda!' the King sententiously exclaimed . . . 'She would have little, or maybe nothing, to wear,' he clairvoyantly went on. 'I see her standing shivering, waiting for Yousef . . . Chained by the leg, perhaps, exposed to the howling winds.'*

'Nonsense. She means to say she can't get away yet on account of her engagements; that's all.'

'After Cowes-week,' Lady Something put in, 'she is due to pay a round of visits before joining her parents in the North.'

'How I envy her,' the Archduchess sighed, 'amid that entrancing scene . . .'

Lady Something looked *attendrie*.

'Your Royal Highness is attached to England?' she asked.

'I fear I was never there . . . But I shall always remember I put my

---

* *Winds*, pronounced as we're told 'in poetry'.

hair up when I was twelve years old because of the Prince of Wales.'

'Oh? And . . . which of the Georges?' Lady Something gasped.

'It's so long ago now that I really forget.'

'And pray, ma'am, what was the point of it?'

The Archduchess chuckled.

'Why, so as to look eligible of course!' she replied, returning to her knitting.

Amid the general flutter following the King's appearance it was easy enough for the Duchess of Varna to slip away. Knowing the palace inside out it was unnecessary to make any fuss. Passing through a long room, where a hundred holland-covered chairs stood grouped, Congresswise, around a vast table, she attained the Orangery, that gave access to the drive. The mellay of vehicles had considerably increased, and the Duchess paused a moment to consider which she should borrow when, recollecting she wished to question one of the royal gardeners on a little matter of mixing manure, she decided to return through the castle grounds instead. Taking a path that descended between rhododendrons and grim old cannons towards the town, she was comparing the capriciousness of certain bulbs to that of certain people when she heard her name called from behind and, glancing round, perceived the charming silhouette of the Countess of Tolga.

'I couldn't stand it inside. Could you?'

'My *dear*, what a honeymoon hat!'

'It was made by me!'

'Oh, Violet . . .' the Duchess murmured, her face taking on a look of wonder.

'Don't forget, dear, Sunday.'

'Is it a party?'

'I've asked Grim-lips and Ladybird, Hairy and Fluffy, Hardylegs and Bluewings, Spindleshanks and Our Lady of Furs.'

'Not Nanny-goat?'

'Luckily . . .' the Countess replied, raising to her nose the heliotropes in her hand.

'Is he no better?'

'You little know, dear, what it is to be all alone with him chez soi when he thinks and sneers into the woodwork.'

Into the woodwork?

'He addresses the ceiling, the walls, the floor – me never!'

'Dear dove.'

'All I can I'm plastic.'

'Can one be plastic ever enough, dear?'

'Often but for Olga . . .' the Countess murmured, considering a little rosy ladybird on her arm.

'I consider her ever so compelling, ever so wistful –' the Duchess of Varna averred.

'Sweet girl –! She's just my consolation.'

'She reminds me, does she you? of that *Miss Hobart* in de Grammont's *Memoirs*.'

'C'est une âme exquise!'

'Well, au revoir, dear: we shall meet again at the Princess Leucippe's later on,' the duchess said, detecting her gardener in the offing.

By the time she had obtained her recipe and cajoled a few special shoots from various exotic plants, the sun had begun to decline. Emerging from the palace by a postern-gate, where lounged a sentry, she found herself almost directly beneath the great acacias on the Promenade. Under the lofty leafage of the trees, as usual towards this hour, society in its varying grades had congregated to be gazed upon. Mounted on an eager-headed little horse, his Weariness (who loved being seen) was plying up and down, while in his wake a *'screen artiste'*, on an Arabian mare with powdered withers and eyes made up with kohl, was creating a sensation. Every time she used her whip the powder rose in clouds. Wending her way through the throng the duchess recognised the rose-harnessed horses of Countess Medusa Rappa – the Countess bolt upright, her head carried stiffly staring with a pathetic expression of dead *joie-de-vie* between her coachman's and footman's waists. But the intention of calling at the Café Cleopatra caused the duchess to hasten. The possibility of learning something beneficial to herself was a lure not to be resisted. Pausing to allow the marvellous blue automobile of Count Ann-Jules to pass (with the dancer Kalpurnia inside), she crossed the Avenue, where there seemed, on the whole, to be fewer people. Here she remarked a little ahead of her the masculine form of the Countess Yvorra, taking a quiet stroll before *Salut* in the company of her Confessor. In the street she usually walked with her hands clasped behind her back, huddled up like a statesman. '*Des choses abominables! . . . Des choses hors nature!*' she was saying, in tones of evident relish, as the duchess passed.

Meanwhile Madame Wetme was seated anxiously by the samovar in her drawing-room. To receive the duchess, she had assumed a mashlak à la mode, whitened her face and rouged her ears, and set a small but costly aigrette at an insinuating angle in the edifice of her hair. As the hour of Angelus approached the tension of waiting grew more and more acute, and beneath the strain of expectation even the little iced-sugar cakes upon the tea-table looked green with worry.

Suppose, after all, she shouldn't come? Suppose she had already left? Suppose she were in prison? Only the other day a woman of the highest fashion, a leader of 'society' with an *A*, had served six months as a consequence of her extravagance . . .

In agitation Madame Wetme helped herself to a small glassful of *Cointreau* (her favourite liqueur), when, feeling calmer for the consommation, she was moved to take a peep out of Antoine.

But nobody chic at all met her eye.

Between the oleanders upon the curb, that rose up darkly against a flame-pink sky, two young men dressed 'as poets' were arguing and gesticulating freely over a bottle of beer. Near them, a sailor with a blue dropping collar and dusty boots (had he walked, poor wretch, to see his mother?) was gazing stupidly at the large evening gnats that revolved like things bewitched about the café lamps, while below the window a lean soul in glasses, evidently an impresario, was loudly exclaiming: 'London has robbed me of my throat, sir!! It has deprived me of my voice.'

No, an 'off' night certainly!

Through a slow, sun-flower of a door (that kept on revolving long after it had been pushed) a few military men bent on a game of billiards, or an early *fille de joie* (only the discreetest *des filles* '*serieuses*' were supposed to be admitted), came and went.

'Tonight they're fit for church,' Madame Wetme complacently smiled as the door swung round again. 'Navy-blue and silver-fox looks the goods,' she reflected, 'upon any occasion! It suggests something sly – like a nurse's uniform.'

'A lady in the drawing-room, Madame, desires to speak to you,' a chasseur tunefully announced, and fingering nervously her aigrette Madame Wetme followed.

The Duchess of Varna was inspecting a portrait with her back to the door as her hostess entered.

'I see you're looking at my Murillo!' Madame Wetme began.

'Oh . . . Is it o-ri-gi-nal?' the duchess drawled.

'No.'

'I *thought* not.'

'To judge by the bankruptcy-sales of late (and it's curious how many there've been . . .), it would seem, from the indifferent figure he makes, that he is no longer accounted chic,' Madame Wetme observed as she drew towards the duchess a chair.

'I consider the chic to be such a very false religion! . . .' the duchess said, accepting the seat which was offered her.

'Well, I come of an old Huguenot family myself!'

'— . . . ?'

'Ah, my early home . . . Now, I hear, it's nothing but a weed-crowned ruin.'

The duchess considered the ivory cat handle of her parasol. 'You wrote to me?' she asked.

'Yes: about the coming court.'

'About it?'

'Every woman has her dream, duchess! And mine's to be presented.'

'The odd ambition!' the duchess crooned.

'I admit we live in the valley. Although *I* have a great sense of the hills!' Madame Wetme declared demurely.

'Indeed?'

'My husband, you see . . .'

'. . . . .'

'Ah! well!'

'Of course.'

'If I'm not asked this time, I shall die of grief.'

'Have you made the request before?'

'I have attempted!'

'Well?'

'When the Lord Chamberlain refused me, I shed tears of blood,' Madame Wetme wanly retailed.

'It would have been easier, no doubt, in the late king's time!'

Madame Wetme took a long sighing breath.

'I only once saw him in my life,' she said, 'and then he was standing against a tree, in an attitude offensive to modesty.'

'Tell me . . . as a public man, what has your husband done –'

'His money helped to avert, I always contend, the noisy misery of a War!'

'He's open-handed?'

'Ah . . . as you would find . . .'

The duchess considered. 'I *might*,' she said, 'get you cards for a State concert . . .'

'A State concert, duchess? That's no good to me!'

'A drawing-room you know is a very dull affair.'

'I will liven it!'

'Or an invitation perhaps to begin with to one of the Embassies – the English for instance might lead . . .'

'Nowhere . . . ! You can't depend on that: people have asked me to lunch, and left me to pay for them . . . ! There is so much trickery in Society . . .' Madame Wetme laughed.

The duchess smiled quizzically. 'I forget if you know the Tolgas,' she said.

'By "name"!'

'The Countess is more about the throne at present than I.'

'Possibly – but oh *you* who do *everything*, duchess?' Madame Wetme entreated.

'I suppose there are things still one wouldn't do however –!' the duchess took offence.

'The Tolgas are so hard.'

'You want a misfortune and they're sweet to you. Successful persons they're positively hateful to!'

'These women of the bedchamber are all alike so glorified. You would never credit they were chambermaids at all! I often smile to myself when I see one of them at a *première* at the Opera, gorged with pickings, and think that, most likely, but an hour before she was stumbling along a corridor with a pailful of slops!'

'You're fond of music, Madame?' the duchess asked.

'It's my joy: I could go again and again to *The Blue Banana!*'

'I've not been.'

'Pom-pom, pompity-pom! We might go one night, perhaps, together.'

'. . .'

'Doudja Degdeg is always a draw, although naturally now she is getting on!'

'And I fear so must I' – the duchess rose remarking.

'So soon?'

'I'm only so sorry I can't stay longer –!'

'Then it's all decided,' Madame Wetme murmured archly as she pressed the bell.

'Oh, I'd not say that.'

'If I'm not asked, remember, this time, I shall die with grief.'

'Tonight the duke and I are dining with the Leucippes, and possibly . . .' the duchess broke off to listen to the orchestra in the café below, which was playing the waltz-air from *Der Rosenkavalier*.

'They play well!' she commented.

'People often tell me so.'

'It must make one restless, dissatisfied, that yearning, yearning music continually at the door!'

Madame Wetme sighed.

'It makes you often long,' she said, 'to begin your life again!'

'Again?'

'Really it's queer I came to yoke myself with a man so little fine . . .'

'Still –! If he's open-handed,' the duchess murmured as she left the room.

IV

One grey, unsettled morning (it was the first of June) the English Colony of Kairoulla* awoke in arms. It usually did when the Embassy entertained. But the omissions of the Ambassador were, as old Mr Ladboyson, the longest-established member of the colony, declared, 'not to be fathomed', and many of those overlooked declared they should go all the same. Why should Mrs Montgomery (who, when all was said and done, was nothing but a governess) be invited and not Mrs Barleymoon who was 'nothing' (in the most distinguished sense of the word) at all? Mrs Barleymoon's position, as a captain's widow with means, unquestionably came before Mrs Montgomery's, who drew a salary and hadn't often an h.

Miss Grizel Hopkins, too – the cousin of an Earl, and Mrs Bedley the 'Mother' of the English Colony, both had been ignored. It was true Ann Bedley kept a circulating library and a tea-room combined and gave 'Information' to tourists as well (a thing she had done these forty years), but was that a sufficient reason why she should be totally taboo? *No*; in old Lord Clanlubber's time all had been made welcome and there had been none of these heartburnings at all. Even the Irish coachman of the Archduchess was known to have been received – although it had been outside of course upon the lawn. Only gross carelessness, it was felt, on the part of those attachés could account for the extraordinary present neglect.

'I don't myself mind much,' Mrs Bedley said, who was seated over a glass of morning milk and 'a plate of fingers' in the *Circulating* end of the shop: 'going out at night upsets me. And the last time Dr Babcock was in he warned me not.'

'What is the Embassy there for but to be hospitable?' Mrs

* The Capital of Pisuerga.

Barleymoon demanded from the summit of a ladder, where she was choosing herself a book.

'You're showing your petticoat, dear – excuse me telling you,' Mrs Bedley observed.

'When will you have something new, Mrs Bedley?'

'Soon, dear . . . soon.'

'It's always "soon",' Mrs Barleymoon complained.

'Are you looking for anything, Bessie, in particular?' a girl, with loose blue eyes that did not seem quite firm in her head, and a literary face, inquired.

'No, only something,' Mrs Barleymoon replied, 'I've not had before and before and before.'

'By the way, Miss Hopkins,' Mrs Bedley said, 'I've to fine you for pouring tea over *My Stormy Past*.'

'It was coffee, Mrs Bedley – not tea.'

'Never mind, dear, what it was, the charge for a stain is the same as you know,' Mrs Bedley remarked, turning to attend to Mrs Montgomery who, with his Naughtiness, Prince Olaf, had entered the Library.

'Is it in?' Mrs Montgomery mysteriously asked.

Mrs Bedley assumed her glasses.

'*Mmnops*,' she replied, peering with an air of secretiveness in her private drawer where she would sometimes reserve or 'hold back' a volume for a subscriber who happened to be in her special good graces.

'I've often said,' Mrs Barleymoon from her ladder sarcastically let fall, 'that Mrs Bedley has her pets!'

'You are all my pets, my dear,' Mrs Bedley softly cooed.

'Have you read *Men – my Delight*, Bessie?' Miss Hopkins asked, 'by Cora Velasquez.'

'No!'

'It's not perhaps a very . . . It's about two dark, and three fair, men,' she added vaguely.

'Most women's novels seem to run off the rails before they reach the end, and I'm not very fond of them,' Mrs Barleymoon said.

'And anyway, dear, it's out,' Mrs Bedley asserted.

'*The Passing of Rose* I read the other day,' Mrs Montgomery said, 'and *so* enjoyed it.'

'Isn't that one of Ronald Firbank's books?'

'No, dear, I don't think it is. But I never remember an author's name and I don't think it matters!'

'I suppose I'm getting squeamish! But this Ronald Firbank I can't take to at all. *Valmouth!* Was there ever a novel more coarse? I assure you I hadn't gone very far when I had to put it down.'

'It's *out*,' Mrs Bedley suavely said, 'as well,' she added, 'as the rest of them.'

'I once met him,' Miss Hopkins said, dilating slightly the *retinae* of her eyes. 'He told me writing books was by no means easy!'

Mrs Barleymoon shrugged.

'Have you nothing more enthralling, Mrs Bedley,' she persuasively asked, 'tucked away?'

'Try *The Call of the Stage*, dear,' Mrs Bedley suggested.

'You forget, Mrs Bedley,' Mrs Barleymoon replied, regarding solemnly her *crêpe*.

'Or *Mary of the Manse*, dear.'

'I've read *Mary of the Manse* twice, Mrs Bedley – and I don't propose to read it again.'

'. . . . . ?'

'. . . . . !'

Mrs Bedley became abstruse.

'It's dreadful how many poets take to drink,' she reflected.

A sentiment to which her subscribers unanimously assented.

'I'm taking *Men are Animals*, by the Hon. Mrs Victor Smythe, and *What Every Soldier Ought to Know*, Mrs Bedley,' Miss Hopkins breathed.

'And I *The East is Whispering*,' Mrs Barleymoon in hopeless tones affirmed.

'Robert Hitchinson! He's a good author.'

'Do you think so? I feel his books are all written in hotels with the bed unmade at the back of the chair.'

'And I dare say you're right, my dear.'

'Well, Mrs Bedley, I must go – if I want to walk to my husband's grave,' Mrs Barleymoon declared.

'Poor Bessie Barleymoon,' Mrs Bedley sighed, after Mrs Barleymoon and Miss Hopkins had gone: 'I fear she frets!'

'We all have our trials, Mrs Bedley.'

'And some more than others.'

'Court life, Mrs Bedley, it's a funny thing.'

'It looks as though we may have an English Queen, Mrs Montgomery.'

'I don't believe it!'

'Most of the daily prints I see are devoting leaders to the little dog the Princess Elsie sent out the other day.'

'Odious, ill-mannered, horrid little beast . . .'

'It seems, dear, he ran from room to room looking for her until he came to the prince's door, where he just lay down and whined.'

'And what does that prove, Mrs Bedley?'

'I really don't know, Mrs Montgomery. But the press seemed to find it "significant",' Mrs Bedley replied as a Nun of the Flaming-Hood with a jolly face all gold with freckles entered the shop.

'Have you *Valmouth* by Ronald Firbank or *Inclinations* by the same author?' she asked.

'Neither, I'm sorry – both are out!'

'Maladetta ✠✠✠✠ ! But I'll be passing soon again,' the Sister answered as she twinklingly withdrew.

'You'd not think now by the look of her she had been at Girton!' Mrs Bedley remarked.

'Once a Girton girl always a Girton girl, Mrs Bedley.'

'It seems a curate drove her to it . . .'

'I'm scarcely astonished. Looking back, I remember the average curate at home as something between a eunuch and a snigger.'

'Still, dear, I could never renounce my religion. As I said to the dear Chaplain only the other day (while he was having some tea), Oh, if only I were a man, I said! Wouldn't I like to *denounce* the disgraceful goings-on every Sabbath down the street at the church of the Blue Jesus.'

'And I assure you it's positively *nothing*, Mrs Bedley, at the

Jesus, to what it is at the church of St Mary the Fair! I was at the wedding of one of the equerries lately, and never saw anything like it.'

'It's about time there was an English wedding, in *my* opinion, Mrs Montgomery!'

'There's not been one in the Colony indeed for some time.'

Mrs Bedley smiled undaunted.

'I trust I may be spared to dance before long at Dr and Mrs Babcock's!' she exclaimed.

'Kindly leave Cunnie out of it, Mrs Bedley,' Mrs Montgomery begged.

'So it's Cunnie already you call him!'

'Dr Cuncliffe and I scarcely meet.'

'People talk of the immense sameness of marriage, Mrs Montgomery; but all the same, my dear, a widow's not much to be envied.'

'There are times, it's true, Mrs Bedley, when a woman feels she needs fostering; but it's a feeling she should try to fight against.'

'Ah, my dear, I never could resist *a mon!*' Mrs Bedley exclaimed.

Mrs Montgomery sighed.

'Once,' she murmured meditatively, 'men (those procurers of delights) engaged me utterly . . . I was their *slave* . . . Now . . . One does not burn one's fingers twice, Mrs Bedley.'

Mrs Bedley grew introspective.

'My poor husband sometimes would be a little frightening, a little fierce . . . at night, my dear, especially. Yet how often now I miss him!'

'You're better off as you are, Mrs Bedley, believe me,' Mrs Montgomery declared, looking round for his Naughtiness, who was amusing himself on the library-steps.

'You must find him a handful to educate, my dear.'

'It will be a relief *indeed*, Mrs Bedley, when he goes to Eton!'

'I'm told so long as a boy is grounded . . .'

'His English accent is excellent, Mrs Bedley, and he shows quite a talent for languages,' Mrs Montgomery assured.

'I'm delighted, I'm sure, to hear it!'

'Well, Mrs Bedley, I mustn't stand dawdling: I've to 'ave my 'air shampooed and waved for the Embassy party tonight you know!' And taking his Naughtiness by the hand, the royal governess withdrew.

V

Among those attached to the Chedorlahomor expedition was a young – if thirty-five be young – eccentric Englishman from Wales, the Hon. 'Eddy' Monteith, a son of Lord Intriguer. Attached first to one thing and then another, without ever being attached to any, his life had been a gentle series of attachments all along. But this new attachment was surely something better than a temporary secretary-ship to a minister, or 'aiding' an ungrateful general, or waiting in through draughts (so affecting to the constitution) in the ante-rooms of hard-worked royalty, in the purlieus of Pall Mall. Secured by the courtesy of his ex-chief, Sir Somebody Something, an old varsity friend of his father, the billet of 'surveyor and occasional help' to the Chedorlahomorian excavation party had been waywardly accepted by the Hon. 'Eddy' just as he had been upon the point of attaching himself, to the terror of his relatives and the amusement of his friends, to a monastery of the Jesuit Order as a likely candidate for the cowl.

Indeed he had already gone so far as to sit to an artist for his portrait in the habit of a monk, gazing ardently at what looked to be the Escurial itself, but in reality was nothing other than an 'impression' from the kitchen garden of Intriguer Park. And now this sudden change, this call to the East instead. There had been no time, unfortunately, before setting out to sit again in the picturesque 'sombrero' of an explorer, but a ready camera had performed miracles, and the relatives of the Hon. 'Eddy' were relieved to behold his smiling countenance in the illustrated weeklies, pick in hand, or with one foot resting on his spade while examining a broken jar, with just below the various editors' comments: *To join the Expedition to Chedorlahomor – the Hon. 'Eddy' Monteith, only son of Lord Intriguer; or, Off to Chedorlahomor! or, Bon Voyage . . . !*

Yes, the temptation of the expedition was not to be withstood, and for vows and renunciations there was always time! . . . And now, leaning idly on his window ledge in a spare room of the Embassy, while his man unpacked, he felt, as he surveyed the distant dome of the Blue Jesus above the dwarf-palm trees before the house, half-way to the East already. He was suffering a little in his dignity from the contretemps of his reception; for, having arrived at the Embassy among a jobbed troop of serfs engaged for the night, he had at first been mistaken by Lady Something for one of them. 'The cloak-room will be in the smoking-room!' she had said, and in spite of her laughing excuses and ample apologies he could not easily forget it. What was there in his appearance that could conceivably recall a cloak-room attendant –? *He* who had been assured he had the profile of a 'Rameses'! And going to a mirror he scanned, with less per-haps than his habitual contentment, the light, liver-tinted hair, grey narrow eyes, hollow cheeks, and pale mouth like a broken moon. He was looking just a little fatigued, he fancied, from his journey, and, really, it was all his hostess deserved, if he didn't go down.

'I have a headache, Mario,' he told his man (a Neapolitan who had been attached to almost as many professions as his master). 'I shall not leave my room! Give me a kimono: I will take a bath.'

Undressing slowly, he felt, as the garments dropped away, he was acting properly in refraining from attending the soirée, and only hoped the lesson would not be 'lost' on Lady Something, who, he feared, must be incurably dense.

Lying amid the dissolving bath crystals while his man-servant deftly bathed him, he fell into a sort of coma, sweet as a religious trance. Beneath the rhythmic sponge, perfumed with *Kiki*, he was St Sebastian, and as the water became cloudier, and the crystals evaporated amid the steam, he was Teresa . . . and he would have been, most likely, the Blessed Virgin herself but that the bath grew gradually cold.

'You're looking a little pale, sir, about the gills!' the valet solicitously observed, as he gently dried him.

The Hon. 'Eddy' winced. 'I forbid you ever to employ the word gill, Mario,' he exclaimed. 'It is inharmonious, and in English it jars; whatever it may do in Italian.'

'Overtired, sir, was what I meant to say.'

'Basta!' his master replied, with all the brilliant glibness of the Berlitz-school.

Swathed in towels, it was delicious to relax his powder-blanched limbs upon a comfy couch, while Mario went for dinner: 'I don't care what it is! So long as it isn't –' (naming several dishes that he particularly abhorred, or might be 'better', perhaps, without) – 'And be sure, fool, not to come back without champagne.'

He could not choose but pray that the Ambassadress had nothing whatever to do with the Embassy cellar, for from what he had seen of her already he had only a slight opinion of her discernment.

Really he might have been excused had he taken her to be the cook instead of the social representative of the Court of St James, and he was unable to repress a caustic smile on recollecting her appearance that afternoon, with her hat awry, crammed with *Maréchal Niel* roses, hot, and decoiffed, flourishing a pair of garden-gauntlets, as she issued her commands. What a contrast to his own Mamma – 'so different', . . . and his thoughts returned to Intriguer – 'dear Intriguer, . . .' that, if only to vex his father's ghost, he would one day turn into a Jesuit college! The Confessional should be fitted in the paternal study, and engravings of the Inquisition, or the sweet faces of Lippi and Fra Angelico, replace the Agrarian certificates and tiresome trophies of the chase; while the crack of the discipline in Lent would echo throughout the house! How 'useful' his friend Robbie Renard would have been. But alas poor Robbie; he had passed through life at a rapid canter, having died at nineteen . . .

Musingly he lit a cigarette. Through the open window a bee droned in on the blue air of evening. Closing his eyes he fell to considering whether the bee of one country would understand the remarks of that of another. The effect of the soil of a nation, had it consequences upon its flora? Were plants influenced at their roots? People sometimes spoke (and especially ladies) of the language of flowers . . . the pollen therefore of an English rose would probably vary, not inconsiderably, from that of a French, and a bee born and bred at home (at *Intriguer*, for instance) would be at a loss to understand (it clearly followed) the conversation of one born and bred, here, abroad. A bee's idiom varied then, as did man's! And he wondered, this being proved the case, where the best bees' accents were generally acquired . . .

Opening his eyes, he perceived his former school chum, Lionel Limpness – Lord Tiredstock's third (and perhaps most gifted) son, who was an honorary attaché at the Embassy – standing over him, his spare figure already arrayed in an evening suit.

'Sorry to hear you're off colour, Old Dear!' he exclaimed, sinking down upon the couch beside his friend.

'I'm only a little shaken, Lionel . . .: have a cigarette.'

'And so you're off to Chedorlahomor, Old Darling?' Lord Tiredstock's third son said.

'I suppose so . . .' the only son of Lord Intriguer replied.

'Well, I wish I was going too!'

'It would be charming, Lionel, of course to have you: but they might appoint you Vice-Consul at Sodom, or something?'

'Why *Vice*? Besides . . . ! There's no consulate there yet,' Lord Tirestock's third son said, examining the objects upon the portable altar, draped in prelatial purple, of his friend.

'Turn over, Old Dear, while I chastise you!' he exclaimed, waving what looked to be a tortoiseshell lorgnon to which had been attached three threads of 'cerulean' floss silk.

'Put it down, Lionel, and don't be absurd.'

'Over we go. Come on.'

'Really, Lionel.'

'Penitence! To thy knees, Sir!'

And just as it seemed that the only son of Lord Intriguer was to be deprived of all his towels, the Ambassadress mercifully entered.

'*Poor* Mr Monteith!' she exclaimed in tones of concern, bustling forward with a tablespoon and a bottle containing physic, '*so* unfortunate . . . Taken ill at the moment you arrive! But Life is like that!'

Clad in the flowing circumstance of an oyster satin ball-dress, and all a-glitter like a Christmas tree (with jewels), her arrival perhaps saved her guest a 'whipping'.

'Had I known, Lady Something, I was going to be ill, I would have gone to the Ritz!' the Hon. 'Eddy' gasped.

'And you'd have been bitten all over!' Lady Something replied.

'Bitten all over?'

'The other evening we were dining at the Palace, and I heard the dear King say – but I oughtn't to talk and excite you –'

'By the way, Lady Something,' Lord Tiredstock's third son asked: 'what is the etiquette for the Queen of Dateland's eunuch?'

'It's all according; but you had better ask Sir Somebody, Mr Limpness,' Lady Something replied, glancing with interest at the portable altar.

'I've done so, and he declared he'd be jiggered!'

'I recollect in Pera when we occupied the Porte, they seemed (those of the old Grand Vizier – oh what a good-looking man he was –! such eyes –! and such a *way* with him –! *Despot!!*) only too thankful to crouch in corners.'

'Attention with that castor-oil . . . !'

'It's not castor-oil; it's a little decoction of my own, – aloes, gregory, a dash of liquorice. And the rest is buckthorn!'

'Euh!'

'It's not so bad, though it mayn't be very nice . . . Toss it off like a brave man, Mr Monteith (nip his nostrils, Mr Limpness), and while he takes it, I'll offer a silent prayer for him at that duck of an altar,' and, as good as her word, the Ambassadress made towards it.

'You're altogether too kind,' the Hon. 'Eddy' murmured, seeking refuge in a book – a volume of *Juvenalia* published for him by 'Blackwood of Oxford', and becoming absorbed in its contents: 'Ah Doris' – 'Lines to Doris' – 'Lines to Doris: written under the influence of wine, sun and fever' – 'Ode to Swinburne' – 'Sad Tamarisks' – 'Rejection' – 'Doigts Obscènes' – 'They Call me *Lily!!*' – 'Land of Titian! Land of Verdi! O Italy!' – 'I heard the Clock:

> I heard the clock strike seven,
> Seven strokes I heard it strike!
> His Lordship's gone to London
> And won't be back to night.'

He had written it at Intriguer, after a poignant domestic disagreement, his Papa, – the 'his lordship' of the poem – had stayed away, however, considerably longer . . . And here was a sweet thing suggested by an old Nursery Rhyme, 'Loves, have you Heard?'

> 'Loves, have you heard about the rabbits??
> They have such odd fantastic habits . . .
> Oh, Children . . . ! I daren't disclose to You
> The licentious things *some* rabbits do.'

I had 'come to him' quite suddenly out ferreting one day with the footman . . .

But a loud crash as the portable altar collapsed beneath the weight of the Ambassadress aroused him unpleasantly from his thoughts.

'Horrid dangerous thing!' she exclaimed as Lord Tiredstock's third son assisted her to rise from her 'Silent' prayer: 'I had no idea it wasn't solid! But Life is like that . . .' she added somewhat wildly.

'Pity O my God! Deliver me!' the Hon. 'Eddy' breathed, but the hour of *deliverance* it seemed was not just yet; for at that instant the Hon. Mrs Chilleywater, the 'literary' wife of the first attaché, thrust her head in at the door.

'How are you?' she asked. 'I thought perhaps I might find *Harold* . . .'

'He's with Sir Somebody.'

'Such mysteries!' Lady Something said.

'This betrothal of Princess Elsie's is simply wearing him out,' Mrs Chilleywater declared, sweeping the room with half-closed, expressionless eyes.

'It's a pity you can't pull the strings for us,' Lady Something ventured: 'I was saying so lately to Sir Somebody.'

'I wish I could, dear Lady Something: I wouldn't mind wagering I'd soon bring it off!'

'Have you fixed up Grace Gillstow yet, Mrs Chilleywater?' Lord Tiredstock's third son asked.

'She shall marry Baldwin: but not before she has been seduced first by Barnaby . . .'

'What are you talking about?' the Hon. 'Eddy' queried.

'Of Mrs Chilleywater's forthcoming book.'

'Why should Barnaby get Grace –? Why not Tex?'

But Mrs Chilleywater refused to enter into reasons.

'She is looking for cowslips,' she said, 'and oh I've such a wonderful description of a field of cowslips . . . They make quite a darling setting for a powerful scene of lust.'

'So Grace loses her virtue!' Lord Tiredstock's third son exclaimed.

'Even so she's far too good for Baldwin: after the underhand shabby way he behaved to Charlotte, Kate, and Millicent!'

'Life is like that, dear,' the Ambassadress blandly observed.

'It ought not to be, Lady Something!' Mrs Chilleywater looked vindictive.

Née Victoria Gellybore Frinton, and the sole heir of Lord Seafairer of Sevenelms, Kent, Mrs Harold Chilleywater, since her marriage 'for Love', had developed a disconcerting taste for fiction – a taste that was regarded at the Foreign Office with disapproving forbearance . . . So far her efforts (written under her maiden name in full with her husband's as well appended) had been confined to lurid studies of low life (of which she knew nothing at all); but the Hon. Harold Chilleywater had been gently warned that if he was not to remain at Kairoulla until the close of his career the style of his wife must really grow less *virile*.

'I agree with V.G.F.,' the Hon. Lionel Limpness murmured, fondling meditatively his 'Charlie Chaplin' moustache – 'Life ought not to be.'

'It's a mistake to bother oneself over matters that can't be remedied.'

Mrs Chilleywater acquiesced. 'You're right indeed, Lady Something,' she said, 'but I'm so sensitive . . . I seem to *know* when I talk to a man the colour of his braces . . . ! I say to myself: "Yours are violet . . ." "Yours are blue . . ." "His are red . . ."'

'I'll bet you anything, Mrs Chilleywater, you like, you won't guess what mine are,' the Hon. Lionel Limpness said.

'I should say, Mr Limpness, that they were *multi-hued* – like Jacob's,' Mrs Chilleywater replied, as she withdrew her head.

The Ambassadress prepared to follow.

'Come, Mr Limpness,' she exclaimed, 'we've exhausted the poor fellow quite enough – and besides, here comes his dinner.'

'Open the champagne, Mario,' his master commanded immediately they were alone.

'"Small" beer is all the butler would allow, sir.'

'Damn the b . . . butler!'

'What he calls a *demi-brune*, sir. In Naples we say *spumanti!*'

'To — with it.'

'Non é tanto amarro, sir; it's more sharp, as you'd say, than bitter . . .'

'. . . . . . ! ! ! ! ! !'

And language *unmonastic* far into the night reigned supreme.

Standing beneath the portraits of King Geo and Queen Glory, Lady Something, behind a large sheaf of mauve malmaisons, was growing stiff. Already, for the most part, the guests were welcomed, and it was only the Archduchess now, who as usual was late, that kept their Excellencies lingering at the head of the stairs. Her Majesty Queen Thleeanouhee of the Land of Dates had just arrived, but seemed loath to leave the stairs, while her hostess, whom she addressed affectionately as her *dear gazelle*, remained upon them – 'Let us go away by and by, my dear gazelle,' she exclaimed with a primitive smile, 'and remove our corsets and talk.'

'Unhappily Pisuerga is not the East, ma'am!' Lady Something replied.

'Never mind, my dear; we will introduce this innovation . . .'

But the arrival of the Archduchess Elizabeth spared the Ambassadress from what might too easily have become an 'incident'.

In the beautiful chandeliered apartments several young couples were pirouetting to the inevitable waltz from the Blue Banana, but most of the guests seemed to prefer exploring the conservatories and winter garden, or elbowing their way into a little room where a new portrait of Princess Elsie had been discreetly placed . . .

'One feels, of course, there *was* a sitting –; but still, it isn't like her!' those that had seen her said.

'The artist has attributed to her at least the pale spent eyes of her father!' the Duchess of Cavaljos remarked to her niece, who was standing quite silent against a rose-red curtain.

Mademoiselle de Nazianzi made no reply. Attaching not the faintest importance to the rumours afloat, still, she could not but feel, at times, a little heart-shaken . . .

The duchess plied her fan.

'She will become florid in time like her mother!' she cheerfully predicted, turning away just as the Archduchess herself approached to inspect the painting.

Swathed in furs, on account of a troublesome cough contracted paddling, she seemed nevertheless in charming spirits.

'Have you been to my new *Pipi?*' she asked.

'Not yet –'

'Oh but you must!'

'I'm told it's even finer than the one at the railway station. Ah, from musing too long on that Hellenic frieze, how often I've missed my train!' the Duchess of Cavaljos murmured, with a little fat deep laugh.

'I have a heavenly idea for another – yellow tiles with thistles . . .'

'Your Royal Highness never repeats herself!'

'Nothing will satisfy me this time,' the Archduchess declared, 'but files of state-documents in all the dear little boxes: in secret, secrets!' she added archly, fixing her eyes on the assembly.

'It's positively pitiable,' the Duchess of Cavaljos commented, 'how the Countess of Tolga is losing her good looks; she has the air tonight of a tired business-woman!'

'She looks at other women as though she would inhale them,' the Archduchess answered, throwing back her furs with a gesture of superb grace, in order to allow her robe to be admired by a lady who was scribbling busily away behind a door, with little nervous lifts of the head. For *noblesse oblige*, and the correspondent of the *Jaw-Waw*, the illustrious Eva Schnerb, was not to be denied.

'Among the many balls of a brilliant season,' the diarist, with her accustomed fluency, wrote, 'none surpassed that which I witnessed at the English Embassy last night. I sat in a corner of the Winter

Garden and literally gorged myself upon the display of dazzling uniforms and jewels. The Ambassadress Lady Something was looking really regal in dawn-white draperies, holding a bouquet of the new mauve malmaisons (which are all the vogue just now), but no one, I thought, looked better than the *Archduchess*, etc. . . . Helping the hostess, I noticed Mrs Harold Chilleywater, in an 'aesthetic' gown of flame-hued Kanitra silk edged with Armousky fur (to possess a dear woolly Armousk as a pet is considered *chic* this season), while over her brain – an intellectual caprice, I wonder? – I saw a tinsel bow . . . She is a daughter of the fortieth Lord Seafairer of Sevenelms Park (so famous for its treasures) and is very artistic and literary having written several novels of English life under her maiden name of Victoria Gellybore-Frinton: – she inherits considerable cleverness *also* from her Mother. Dancing indefatigably (as she always does!), Miss Ivy Something seemed to be thoroughly enjoying her Father's ball: I hear on *excellent authority* there is no foundation in the story of her engagement to a certain young Englishman, said to be bound ere long for the ruins of Sodom and Gomorrah. Among the late arrivals were the Duke and Duchess of Varna – *she* all in golden tissues: they came together with Madame Wetme, who is one of the new hostesses of the season, you know, and they say has bought the Duke of Varna's palatial town-house in Samaden Square –'

'There,' the Archduchess murmured, drawing her wraps about her with a sneeze: 'she has said quite enough now I think about my *toilette!*'

But the illustrious Eva was in unusual fettle, and only closed her notebook towards Dawn, when the nib of her pen caught fire.

VI

And suddenly the Angel of Death passed by and the brilliant season waned. In the Archduchess's bedchamber, watching the antics of priests and doctors, he sat there unmoved. Propped high by many bolsters, in a vast blue canopied bed, the Archduchess lay staring laconically at a diminutive model of a flight of steps, leading to what appeared to be intended, perhaps, as a hall of Attent, off which opened quite a lot of little doors, most of which bore the word: 'Engaged.' A doll, with a ruddy face, in charge, smiled indolently as she sat feigning knitting, suggesting vague 'fleshly thoughts', whenever he looked up, in the Archduchess's spiritual adviser.

And the mind of the sinking woman, as her thoughts wandered, appeared to be tinged with 'matter' too: 'I recollect the first time I heard the *Blue Danube* played!' she broke out: 'it was at Schönnbrunn – schönes Schönnbrunn – My cousin Ludwig of Bavaria came – I wore – the Emperor said –'

'If your imperial highness would swallow this!' Dr Cuncliffe Babcock started forward with a glass.

'Trinquons, trinquons et vive l'amour! Schneider sang that –'

'If your imperial highness –'

'Ah my dear Vienna. Where's Teddywegs?'

At the Archduchess's little escritoire at the foot of the bed her Dreaminess was making ready a few private telegrams, breaking without undue harshness the melancholy news, 'Poor Lizzie has ceased articulating,' she did not think she could improve on that, and indeed had written it several times in her most temperamental hand, when the Archduchess had started suddenly cackling about Vienna.

'*Ssssh*, Lizzie – I never can write when people talk!'

'I want Teddywegs.'

'The Countess Yvorra took him for a run round the courtyard.'

'I think I must undertake a convenience next for dogs . . . It is disgraceful they have not got one already, poor creatures,' the Archduchess crooned, accepting the proffered glass.

'Yes, yes, dear,' the Queen exclaimed, rising and crossing to the window.

The bitter odour of the oleander flowers outside oppressed the breathless air and filled the room as with a faint funereal music. So still a day. Tending the drooping sun-saturated flowers, a gardener with long ivory arms alone seemed animate.

'Pull up your skirt, Marquise! Pull it up . . . It's dragging, a little, in the water.'

'*Judica me, Deus,*' in imperious tones the priest by the bedside besought: '*et discerne causam meam de gente non sancta. Parce, Domine. Parce populo tuo. Ne in aeternum irasceris nobis.*'

'A whale! A whale!'

'*Sustinuit anima mea in verbo ejus, speravit anima mea in Domino.*'

'Elsie?' A look of wonderous happiness overspread the Archduchess's face – She was wading – wading again among the irises and rushes; wading, her hand in Princess Elsie's hand, through a glittering golden sea, towards the wide horizon.

The plangent cry of a peacock rose disquietingly from the garden.

'I'm nothing but nerves, doctor,' her Dreaminess lamented, fidgeting with the crucifix that dangled at her neck upon a chain. *Ultra* feminine, she disliked that another – even *in extremis* – should absorb *all* the limelight.

'A change of scene, ma'am, would be probably beneficial,' Dr Cuncliffe Babcock replied, eyeing askance the Countess of Tolga who unobtrusively entered.

'The couturiers attend your pleasure, ma'am,' in impassive undertones she said, 'to fit your mourning.'

'Oh, tell them the Queen is too tired to try on now,' her Dreaminess answered, repairing in agitation toward a glass.

'They would come here, ma'am,' the Countess said, pointing persuasively to the little ante-room of the Archduchess, where two nuns of the Flaming-Hood were industriously telling their beads.

'– I don't know why, but this glass refuses to flatter me!'

'*Benedicamus Domino! Ostende nobis Domine misericordiam tuam. Et salutare tuum da nobis!*'

'Well, just a toque,' the Queen sadly assented.

'*Indulgentiam absolutionem et remissionem peccatorum nostrorum tribuat nobis omnipotens et misericors Dominus.*'

'Guess who is at the Ritz, ma'am, this week!' the Countess demurely murmured.

'Who is at the Ritz this week, I can't,' the Queen replied.

'*Nobody!*'

'Why, how so?'

'The Ambassadress of England, it seems, has alarmed the world away. I gather they mean to prosecute!'

The Archduchess sighed.

'I want mauve sweet-peas,' she listlessly said.

'Her spirit soars; her thoughts are in the *Champs-Elysées*,' the Countess exclaimed, withdrawing noiselessly to warn the milliners.

'Or in the garden,' the Queen reflected, returning to the window. And she was standing there, her eyes fixed half wistfully upon the long ivory arms of the kneeling gardener, when the Angel of Death (who had sat unmoved throughout the day) arose.

It was decided to fix a period of mourning of fourteen days for the late Archduchess.

VII

Swans and sunlight. A little fishing-boat with coral sails. A lake all grey and green. Beatitude intense. Consummate calm. It was nice to be at the Summer Palace after all.

'The way the air will catch your cheek and make a rose of it,' the Countess of Tolga breathed. And as none of the company heeded her: 'How sweetly the air takes one's cheek,' she sighed again.

The post-prandial exercise of the members of the Court through the palace grounds was almost an institution.

The first half of the mourning prescribed had as yet not run its course, but the tongues of the Queen's ladies had long since made an end of it.

'I hate dancing with a fat man,' Mademoiselle de Nazianzi was saying: 'for if you dance at all near him, his stomach hits you, while if you pull away, you catch either the scent of his breath or the hair of his beard.'

'But, you innocent baby, *all* big men haven't beards,' Countess Medusa Rappa remarked.

'Haven't they? Never mind. Everything's so beautiful,' the young girl inconsequently exclaimed. 'Look at that Thistle! and that Bee! Oh, you darling!'

'Ah, how one's face unbends in gardens!' the Countess of Tolga said, regarding the scene before her with a far-away pensive glance.

Along the lake's shore, sheltered from the winds by a ring of wooded hills, showed many a proud retreat, mirroring its marble terraces to the waveless waters of the lake.

Beneath a twin-peaked crag (known locally as the White Mountain, whose slopes frequently would burst forth into patches of garlic that from the valley resembled snow) nestled the Villa Clement, rented each season by the Ambassador of the Court of St James, while half screened by conifers and rhododendrons, and in

72

the lake itself, was St Helena – the home and place of retirement of a 'fallen' minister of the Crown.

Countess Medusa Rappa cocked her sunshade. 'Whose boat is that,' she asked, 'with the azure oars?'

'It looks nothing but a pea-pod!' the Countess of Tolga declared.

'It belongs to a darling, with delicious lips and eyes like brown chestnuts,' Mademoiselle de Lambèse informed.

'Ah! . . . Ah! . . . Ah! . . . Ah! . . .' her colleagues crooned.

'A sailor?'

The Queen's maid nodded. 'There's a partner, though,' she added, 'a blue-eyed, gashed-cheeked angel . . .'

Mademoiselle de Nazianzi looked away.

'I love the lake with the white wandering ships,' she sentimentally stated, descrying in the distance the prince.

It was usually towards this time, the hour of the siesta, that the lovers would meet and taste their happiness, but today it seemed ordained otherwise.

Before the heir apparent had determined whether to advance or retreat, his father and mother were upon him, attended by two dowagers newly lunched.

'The song of the pilgrim women, how it haunts me,' one of the dowagers was holding forth: 'I could never tire of that beautiful, beautiful music! Never tire of it. Ne-ver . . .'

'Ta, ta, ta, ta,' the Queen vociferated girlishly, slipping her arm affectionately through that of her son.

'How spent you look, my boy . . . Those eyes . . .'

His Weariness grimaced.

'They've just been rubbing in Elsie!' he said.

'Who?'

'"Vasleine" and "Nanny-goat"!'

'Well?'

'Nothing will shake me.'

'What are your objections?'

'She's so extraordinarily uninteresting!'

'Oh, Yousef!' his mother faltered: *do you wish to break my heart?'*

'We had always thought you too lacking in initiative,' King William said (tucking a few long hairs back into his nose), 'to marry against our wishes.'

'They say she walks too wonderfully,' the Queen courageously pursued.

'What? Well?'

'Yes.'

'Thank God for it.'

'And can handle a horse as few others can!'

Prince Yousef closed his eyes.

He had not forgotten how as an undergraduate in England he had come upon the princess once while out with the hounds. And it was only by a consummate effort that he was able to efface the sinister impression she had made – her lank hair falling beneath a man's felt-hat, her habit skirt torn to tatters, her full cheeks smeared in blood – the blood, so it seemed, of her 'first' fox.

A shudder seized him.

'No, nothing can possibly shake me,' he murmured again.

With a detached, cold face, the Queen paused to inhale a rose.

(Oh, you gardens of Palaces . . . ! How often have you witnessed agitation and disappointment? You smooth, adorned paths . . . ! How often have you known the extremes of care . . . ?)

'It would be better to do away I think next year with that bed of cinerarias altogether,' the Queen of Pisuerga remarked, 'since persons won't go round it.'

Traversing the flower plat now, with the air of a black-beetle with a purpose, was the Countess Yvorra.

'We had supposed you higher-principled, Countess,' her sovereign admonished.

The Countess slightly flushed.

'I'm looking for groundsel for my birds, Sire,' she said – 'for my little dickies!'

'We understand your boudoir is a sort of menagerie,' His Majesty affirmed.

The Countess tittered.

'Animals love me,' she archly professed. 'Birds perch on my

breast if only I wave . . . The other day a sweet red robin came and stayed for hours . . . !'

'The Court looks to you to set a high example,' the Queen declared, focusing quizzically a marble shape of Leda green with moss, for whose time-corroded plinth the late Archduchess's toy-terrier was just then showing a certain contempt.

The Countess's long, slightly pulpy fingers strayed nervously towards the rosary at her thigh.

'With your majesty's consent,' she said, 'I propose a campaign to the Island.'

'What? And beard the Count?'

'The salvation of one so fallen, in my estimation should be worth hereafter (at the present rate of exchange, but the values vary) . . . a Plenary perpetual-indulgence: I therefore,' the Countess said, with an upward fleeting glance (and doubtless guileless of intention of irony), 'feel it my *duty* to do what I can.'

'I trust you will take a bodyguard when you go to St Helena?'

'And pray tell Count Cabinet from us,' the King looked implacable, 'we forbid him to serenade the Court this year! or to throw himself into the Lake again or to make himself a nuisance!'

'He was over early this morning, Willie,' the Queen retailed: 'I saw him from a window. Fishing, or feigning to! And with white kid gloves, and a red carnation.'

'Let us catch him stepping ashore!' The King displayed displeasure.

'And as usual the same mignon youth had charge of the tiller.'

'I could tell a singular story of that young man,' the Countess said: 'for he was once a choir-boy at the Blue Jesus. But perhaps I would do better to spare your ears . . .'

'You would do better, a good deal, to spare my cinerarias,' her Dreaminess murmured, sauntering slowly on.

Sun so bright, trees so green, it was a perfect day. Through the glittering fronds of the palms shone the lake like a floor of silver glass strewn with white sails.

'It's odd,' the King observed, giving the dog Teddywegs a sly prod with his cane, 'how he follows Yousef.'

'He seems to know!' the Queen replied.

A remark which so annoyed the Prince that he curtly left the garden.

VIII

But this melancholy period of *crêpe*, a time of idle secrets and unbosomings, was to prove fatal to the happiness of Mademoiselle de Nazianzi. She now heard she was not the first in the Prince's life, and that most of the Queen's maids, indeed, had had identical experiences with her own. She furthermore learned, amid ripples of laughter, of her lover's relations with the Marquesa Pizzi-Parma and of his light dealings with the dancer April Flowers, a negress (to what depths??), at a time when he was enjoying the waxen favours of the wife of his Magnificence the Master of the Horse.

Chilled to the point of numbness, the mortified girl had scarcely winced, and when, on repairing to her room a little later, she had found his Weariness wandering in the corridor on the chance of a surreptitious kiss, she had bolted past him without look or word and sharply closed her door.

The Court had returned to colours when she opened it again, and such had been the trend of her meditations that her initial steps were directed, with deliberate austerity, towards the basilica of the Palace.

Except for the Countess Yvorra, with an *écharpe de décence* drawn over her hair, there was no one in it.

'I thank Thee God for this *escape*,' she murmured, falling to her knees before the silver branches of a cross. 'It is terrible; for I did so love him . . . . and oh how could he ever, with *a negress?* . . . . Pho . . . . I fear this complete upset has

77

considerably aged me . . . .
. . . . But to Thee I cling . . . .
. . . .
. . . .
Preserve me at all times from the toils of the wicked, and forgive
him, as *I* hope to forgive him soon.' Then kindling several candles
with a lingering hand, she shaped her course towards the Kennels,
called Teddywegs to her, and started, with an aching heart, for a
walk.

It was a day of heavy somnolence. Skirting the Rosery, where
gardeners with their slowly moving rakes were tending the sandy
paths, she chose a neglected footway that descended towards the
lake. Indifferent to the vivacity of Teddywegs, who would race on
a little before her, then wait with leonine accouchements of head
until she had almost reached him, when he would prick an ear
and spring forward with a yap of exhortation, she proceeded
leisurely and with many a pause, wrapped in her own mournful
thoughts.

Alack! Among the court circle there was no one to whom in her
disillusion she could look for solace, and her spirit yearned for Sister
Ursula and the Convent of the Flaming-Hood.

Wending her way amid the tall trees, she felt she had never cared
for Yousef as she had for Ursula . . . and broodingly, in order to ease
her heart, she began comparing the two together as she walked
along.

After all, what had he ever said that was not either commonplace
or foolish? Whereas Sister Ursula's talk was invariably pointed, and
often indeed so delicately that words seemed almost too crude a
medium to convey her ethereal meanings, and she would move her
evocative hands, and flash her aura, and it was no fault of hers if you
hadn't a peep of the beyond. And the infinite tenderness of her least
caress! Yousef's lips had seldom conveyed to hers the spell of
Ursula's; and once indeed lately, when he had kissed her, there had
been an unsavoury aroma of tobacco and *charcuterie*, which, to deal
with, had required both tact and courage . . . Ah dear Hood! What
harmony life had held within. Unscrupulous and deceiving men

might lurk around its doors (they often did) coveting the chaste, but Old Jane, the porteress, would open to no man beyond the merest crack. And how right were the nuns in their mistrust of man! Sister Ursula one day had declared, in uplifted mood, that 'marriage was obscene'. Was it –? . . . ?? . . . Perhaps it might be –! How appalling if it was!

She had reached the lake.

Beneath the sky as white as platinum it lay, pearly, dove-like, scintillating capriciously where a heat-shrouded sun kindled its torpid waters into fleeting diamonds. A convulsive breeze strayed gratefully from the opposite shore, descending from the hills that rose up all veiled, and without detail, against the brilliant whiteness of the morning.

Sinking down upon the shingle by an upturned boat, she heaved a brief sigh, and drawing from her vanity-case the last epistles of the Prince, began methodically to arrange them in their proper sequence.

(1) 'What is the matter with my Dearest Girl?'
(2) 'My own tender little Lita, I do not understand –'
(3) 'Darling, what's this –?'
(4) 'Beloved one, I swear –'
(5) 'Your cruel silence –'.

If published in a dainty brochure format about the time of his Coronation they ought to realize no contemptible sum and the proceeds might go to charity, she reflected, thrusting them back again carefully into the bag.

Then, finding the shingle too hard through her thin gown to remain seated long, she got up, and ran a mournful race with Teddywegs along the shore.

Not far along the lake was the 'village', with the Hôtel d'Angleterre et du Lac, its stucco, belettered walls professing: 'Garages, Afternoon Tea, Modern Comfort!' Flitting by this and the unpretentious pier (where long, blonde fishing-nets lay drying in the sun), it was a relief to reach the remoter plage beyond.

Along the banks stretched vast brown carpets of corn and rye, broken by an occasional olive-garth, beneath whose sparse shade the heavy-eyed oxen blinked and whisked their tails, under the attacks of the water-gnats that were swarming around.

Musing on Negresses – and Can-Can dancers in particular – she strolled along a strand all littered with shells and little jewel-like stones.

The sun shone down more fiercely now, and soon, for freshness sake, she was obliged to take to the fields.

Passing among the silver drooping olives, relieved here and there by a stone-pine, or slender cypress-tree eternally green, she sauntered on, often lured aside to pluck the radiant wild-flowers by the way. On the banks the pinkest cyclamens were in bloom, and cornflowers of the hue of paradise, and fine-stemmed poppies flecked with pink.

'Pho! A Negress . . .' she murmured, following the flight of some waterfowl towards the opposite shore.

The mists had fallen from the hills, revealing old woods wrapped in the blue doom of summer.

Beyond those glowing heights, towards this hour, the nuns, each in her cool, shuttered cell, would be immersed in noontide prayer.

'Ursula – for thee!' she sighed, proffering her bouquet in the direction of the town.

A loud splash . . . the sight of a pair of delicate legs (mocking the Law's requirements under the Modesty Act as relating to bathers) . . . Mademoiselle de Nazianzi turned and fled. She had recognized *the Prince.**

* The recollection of this was never quite forgotten.

IX

And in this difficult time of spiritual distress, made more trying perhaps because of the blazing midsummer days and long, pent feverish nights, Mademoiselle de Nazianzi turned in her tribulation towards religion.

The Ecclesiastical set at Court, composed of some six, or so, ex-Circes, under the command of the Countess Yvorra, were only too ready to welcome her, and invitations to meet Monsignor this or 'Father' that, who constantly were being *coaxed* from their musty sacristies and wan-faced acolytes in the capital, in order that they might officiate at Masses, Confessions and Breakfast-parties *à la fourchette*, were lavished daily upon the bewildered girl.

Messages, and hasty informal lightly-pencilled notes, too, would frequently reach her; such as: 'I shall be pouring out cocoa after dinner in bed. Bring your biscuits and join me!' . . . or a rat-a-tat from a round-eyed page and: 'The Countess's comp'ts and she'd take it a Favour if you can make a "Station" with her in chapel later on,' or: 'The Marchioness will be birched tomorrow, and *not* today.'

Oh, the charm, the flavour of the religious world! Where match it for interest or variety!

An emotion approaching sympathy had arisen, perhaps a trifle incongruously, between the injured girl and the Countess Yvorra, and before long, to the amusement of the sceptical element of the Court, the Countess and her Confessor, Father Nostradamus, might often be observed in her society.

'I need a cage-companion, Father, for my little bird,' the Countess one evening said, as they were ambling, all the three of them, before Office up and down the perfectly tended paths: 'ought it to be of the same species and sex, or does it matter? For as I said to myself just now (while listening to a thrush), *All* birds are His creatures.'

The priest discreetly coughed.

81

'Your question requires reflection,' he said. 'What is the bird?'

'A hen canary! – and with a voice, Father! Talk of soul!!'

'H–m . . . a thrush and a canary, I would not myself advise.'

Mademoiselle de Nazianzi tittered.

'Why not let it go?' she asked, turning her eyes towards the window-panes of the palace, that glanced like rows of beaten-gold in the evening sun.

'A hawk might peck it!' the Countess returned, looking up as if for one into a sky as imaginative and as dazzling as Shelley's poetry.

'Even the Court,' Father Nostradamus ejaculated wryly, 'will peck at times.'

The Countess's shoulder-blades stiffened.

'After over thirty years,' she said, 'I find Court life *pathetic* . . .'

'Pathetic?'

'Tragically pathetic . . .'

Mademoiselle de Nazianzi considered wistfully the wayward outline of the hills.

'I would like to escape from it all for a while,' she said, 'and travel.'

'I must hunt you out a pamphlet, by and by, dear child, on the "Dangers of Wanderlust".'

'The Great Wall of China and the Bay of Naples! It seems so frightful never to have seen them!'

'I have never seen the Great Wall, either,' the Countess said, 'and I don't suppose, my dear, I ever shall; though I once did spend a fortnight in Italy.'

'Tell me about it.'

The Countess became reminiscent.

'In Venice,' she said, 'the indecent movements of the gondolieri quite affected my health, and, in consequence, I fell a prey to a sharp nervous fever. My temperature rose and it rose, ah, yes . . . until I became quite ill. At last I said to my maid (she was an English girl from Wales, and almost equally as sensitive as me): "Pack . . . Away!" And we left in haste for Florence. Ah, and Florence, too, I regret to say I found very far from what it ought to have been!!!! I had a window giving on the Arno, and so I could *observe* . . . . I used to see some curious sights! I would not care to scathe your ears, my Innocent, by an inventory of one half of the wantonness that went on; enough to say the tone of the place forced me to fly to Rome, where beneath the shadow of dear St Peter's I grew gradually less distressed.'

'Still, I should like, all the same, to travel!' Mademoiselle de Nazianzi exclaimed, with a sad little snatch of a smile.

'We will ask the opinion of Father Geordie Picpus when he comes again.'

'It would be more fitting,' Father Nostradamus murmured (professional rivalry leaping to his eye), 'if Father Picpus kept himself free of the limelight a trifle more!'

'Often I fear our committees would be corvées without him . . .'

'Tchut.'

'He is very popular . . . too popular, perhaps . . .' the Countess admitted. 'I remember on one occasion, in the Blue Jesus, witnessing the Duchess of Quaranta and Madame Ferdinand Fishbacher fight like wild cats as to which should gain his ear – (any girl might envy Father Geordie his ear) – at Confession next. The odds seemed fairly equal until the Duchess gave the Fishbacher-woman such a violent push – (well down from behind, in the crick of the joints) – that she overturned the confessional box, with Father Picpus within: and when we scared ladies, standing by, had succeeded in dragging him out, he was too shaken, naturally as you can gather, to absolve anyone else *that* day.'

'He has been the object of so many unseemly incidents that one can scarcely recall them all,' Father Nostradamus exclaimed, stooping to pick up a dropped pocket-handkerchief with 'remembrance' knots tied to three of the corners.

'Alas . . . Court life is not uplifting,' the Countess said again, contemplating her muff of *self-made* lace, with a half-vexed forehead. What that muff contained was a constant problem for conjecture; but it was believed by more than one of the maids-in-waiting to harbour 'goody' books and martyrs' bones.

'By generous deeds and Brotherly love,' Father Nostradamus exclaimed, 'we should endeavour to rise above it!'

With the deftness of a virtuoso, the Countess seized, and crushed with her muff, a pale-winged passing gnat.

'Before Life,' she murmured, 'that saddest thing of all, was thrust upon us, I believe I was an angel . . .'

Father Nostradamus passed a musing hand across his brow.

'It may be,' he replied; 'and it very well may be,' he went on, 'that our ante-nativity was a little more brilliant, a little more *h—m* . . . ; and there is nothing unorthodox in thinking so.'

'Oh what did I do then to lose my wings?? What did I ever say to Them?! Father, Father. How did I annoy God? Why did He put me here?'

'My dear child, you ask me things I do not know; but it may be you were the instrument appointed above to lead back to Him our neighbour yonder,' Father Nostradamus answered, pointing with his breviary in the direction of St Helena.

'Never speak to me of that wretched old man.'

For despite the ablest tactics, the most diplomatic angling, Count Cabinet had refused to rally.

'We followed the sails of your skiff today,' Mademoiselle de Nazianzi sighed, 'until the hazes hid them!'

'I had a lilac passage.'

'You delivered the books?'

The Countess shrugged.

'I shall never forget this afternoon,' she said. 'He was sitting in the window over a decanter of wine when I floated down upon him; but no sooner did he see me than he gave a sound like a bleat of a goat, and disappeared: I was determined however to call! There is no bell to the villa, but two bronze door-knockers, well out of reach, are attached to the front-door. These with the ferrule of my parasol I tossed and I rattled, until an adolescent, with bougainvillaea at his ear, came and looked out with an insolent grin, and I recognized Peter Passer from the Blue Jesus grown quite fat.'

'Eh mon Dieu!' Father Nostradamus half audibly sighed.

'Eh mon Dieu . . .' Mademoiselle de Nazianzi echoed, her gaze roving over the palace, whose long window-panes in the setting sun gleamed like sumptuous tissues.

'So that,' the Countess added, 'I hardly propose to venture again.'

'What a site for a Calvary!' Father Nostradamus replied, indicating with a detached and pensive air the cleft in the White Mountain's distant peaks.

'I adore the light the hills take on when the sun drops down,' Mademoiselle de Nazianzi declared.

'It must be close on *Salut* . . .'

It was beneath the dark colonnades by the Court Chapel door that they received the news from the lips of a pair of vivacious dowagers that the Prince was to leave the Summer Palace on the morrow to attend 'the Manoeuvres', after which it was expected his Royal Highness would proceed '*to England*'.

X

And meanwhile the representatives of the Court of St James were enjoying the revivifying country air and outdoor life of the Villa Clement. It was almost exquisite how rapidly the casual mode of existence adopted during the summer villeggiatura by their Excellencies drew themselves and their personnel together, until soon they were as united and as *sans gêne* as the proverbial family party. No mother, in the 'acclimatization' period, could have dosed her offspring more assiduously than did her Excellency the attachés in her charge; flavouring her little inventions frequently with rum or gin until they resembled cocktails. But it was Sir Somebody himself if anyone that required a tonic. Lady Something's pending litigation, involving as it did the crown, was fretting the Ambassador more than he cared to admit, and the Hon. Mrs Chilleywater, ever alert, told 'Harold' that the injudicious chatter of the Ambassadress (who even now, notwithstanding her writ, would say to every other visitor that came to the villa: 'Have you heard about the Ritz? The other night we were dining at the Palace, and I heard the King,' *etc.*) was wearing their old Chief out.

And so through the agreeable vacation life there twitched the grim vein of tension.

Disturbed one day by her daughter's persistent trilling of the latest coster song *When I sees 'im I topple giddy*, Lady Something gathered up her morning letters and stepped out upon the lawn.

Oh so formal, oh so slender towered the cypress-trees against the rose-farded hills and diamantine waters of the lake. The first hint of autumn was in the air; and over the gravel paths, and in the basins of the fountains, a few shed leaves lay hectically strewn already.

Besides an under-stamped missive, with a foreign postmark, from Her Majesty the Queen of the Land of Dates beginning 'My dear Gazel', there was a line from the eloquent and moderately victorious young barrister, engaged in the approaching suit with the Ritz: He had spared himself no pains, he assured his client, in preparing the defence, which was, he said, to be *the respectability of Claridge's*.

'Why bring in Claridge's? . . . ?' the Ambassadress murmured, prodding with the tip of her shoe a decaying tortoiseshell leaf; 'but anyway,' she reflected, 'I'm glad the proceedings fall in winter, as I always look well in furs.'

And mentally she was wrapped in leopard-skins and gazing round the crowded court saluting with a bunch of violets an acquaintance here and there, when her eyes fell on Mrs Chilleywater seated in the act of composition beneath a cedar-tree.

Mrs Chilleywater extended a painful smile of welcome which revealed her pointed teeth and pale-hued gums, repressing, simultaneously, an almost irresistible inclination to murder.

'What! . . . Another writ?' she suavely asked.

'No, dear; but these legal men *will* write . . .'

'I love your defender. He has an air of d'Alembert, sympathetic soul.'

'He proposes pleading Claridge's.'

'Claridge's?'

'Its respectability.'

'Are hotels ever respectable? – I ask you. Though, possibly, the horridest are.'

'Aren't they all horrid!'

'*Natürlich*; but do you know those cheap hotels where the guests are treated like naughty children?'

'No. I must confess I don't,' the Ambassadress laughed.

'Ah, there you are . . .'

Lady Something considered a moment a distant gardener employed in tying chrysanthemum blooms to little sticks.

'I'm bothered about a cook,' she said.

'And I, about a maid! I dismissed ffoliott this morning – well I simply *had* to – for a figure salient.'

'So awkward out here to replace anyone; I'm sure I don't know . . .' the Ambassadress replied, her eyes hovering tragically over the pantaloons strained to splitting point of the stooping gardener.

'It's a pretty prospect . . .'

'Life is a compound!' Lady Something defined it at last.

Mrs Chilleywater turned surprised. 'Not even Socrates,' she declared, 'said anything truer than that.'

'A compound!' Lady Something twittered again.

'I should like to put that into the lips of Delitsiosa.'

'Who's Delitsiosa?' the Ambassadress asked as a smothered laugh broke out beside her.

Mrs Chilleywater looked up.

'I'd forgotten you were there. Strange thing among the cedar-boughs,' she said.

The Hon. Lionel Limpness tossed a slippered foot flexibly from his hammock.

'You may well ask "who's Delitsiosa"!' he exclaimed.

'She is my new heroine,' Mrs Chilleywater replied, after a few quick little clutches at her hair.

'I trust you won't treat her, dear, quite so shamefully as your last.'

The Authoress tittered.

'Delitsiosa is the wife of Marsden Didcote,' she said, 'the manager of a pawnshop in the district of Maida Vale, and in the novel he seduces an innocent seamstress, Iris Drummond, who comes in one day to redeem her petticoat (and really I don't know how I did succeed in drawing the portrait of a little fool!) . . . and when Delitsiosa, her suspicions aroused, can no longer doubt or ignore her husband's intimacy with Iris, already engaged to a lusty young farmer in Kent (some boy) – she decides to yield herself to the entreaties of her brother-in-law Percy, a junior partner in the firm, which brings about the great tussle between the two brothers on the edge of the Kentish cliffs. Iris and Delitsiosa – Iris is anticipating a babelet soon – are watching them from a cornfield, where they're boiling a kettle for afternoon tea; and oh, I've such a darling description of a cornfield. I make you *feel* England!'

'No really, my dear,' Lady Something exclaimed.

'Harold pretends it would be wonderful arranged as an Opera . . . with duos and things and a *Liebestod* for Delitzi towards the close.'

'No, no,' Mr Limpness protested. 'What would become of our modern fiction at all if Victoria Gellybore Frinton gave herself up to the stage?'

'That's quite true, strange thing among the cedar-boughs,' Mrs Chilleywater returned, fingering the floating strings of the band-elette at her brow. 'It's lamentable; yet who is there doing anything at present for English Letters . . . ? Who among us today,' she went on, peering up at him, 'is carrying on the tradition of Fielding? Who really cares? I know *I* do what I can . . . and there's Madam Adrian Bloater, of course. But I can think of no one else; – we two.'

Mr Limpness rocked, critically.

'I can't bear Bloater's books,' he demurred.

'To be frank, neither can I. I'm very fond of Lilian Bloater, I adore her *weltbürgerliche* nature, but I feel like you about her books; I *cannot* read them. If only she would forget Adrian; but she will thrust him headlong into all her work. Have *I* ever drawn Harold? No. (Although many of the public seem to think so!) And please heaven, however *great* my provocation at times may be, I never shall!'

'And there I think you're right,' the Ambassadress answered, frowning a little as the refrain that her daughter was singing caught her ear.

> 'And when I sees 'im
> My heart goes BOOM ! . . .
> And I topple over;
> I topple over, over, over,
> All for Love !'

'I dreamt last night my child was on the Halls.'
'There's no doubt she'd dearly like to be.'
'Her Father would never hear of it!'

'And when she sees me,
Oh when she sees me –
(*The voice slightly false was Harold's*)
Her heart goes BOOM! . . .
And she topples over;
She topples over, over, over,
All for Love!'

'There; they've routed Sir Somebody . . .'

'And when anything vexes him,' Lady Something murmured, appraising the Ambassador's approaching form with a glassy eye, 'he always, you know, blames me!'

Shorn of the sombre, betailed attire, so indispensable for the town-duties of a functionary, Sir Somebody, while rusticating, usually wore a white-twill jacket and black multi-pleated pantaloons; while for headgear he would favour a Mexican sugar-loaf, or green-draped puggaree. 'He looks half-Irish,' Lady Something would sometimes say.

'Infernal Bedlam,' he broke out: 'the house is sheer pandemonium.'

'I found it so too, dear,' Lady Something agreed; 'and so,' she added, removing a fallen tree-bug tranquilly from her hair, 'I've been digesting my letters out here upon the lawn.'

'And no doubt,' Sir Somebody murmured, fixing the placid person of his wife with a keen psychological glance, 'you succeed, my dear, in digesting them?'

'Why shouldn't I?'

'. . .' the Ambassador displayed discretion.

'We're asked to a Lion hunt in the Land of Dates; quite an *entreating* invitation from the dear Queen, – really most pressing and affectionate, – but Princess Elsie's nuptial negotiations and this pending Procès with the Ritz may tie us here for some time.'

'Ah Rosa.'

'Why these constant moans? . . . ? A clairvoyant once told me I'd "the bump of Litigation" – a *cause célèbre* unmistakably defined; so it's as well, on the whole, to have it over.'

'And quite probably; had your statement been correct —'

The Ambassadress gently glowed.

'I'm told it's simply swarming!' she impenitently said.

'Oh Rosa, Rosa . . .'

'And if you doubt it at all, here is an account direct from the Ritz itself,' her Excellency replied, singling out a letter from among the rest. 'It is from dear old General Sir Trotter-Stormer. He says: "I am the only guest here. I must say, however, the attendance is beyond all praise, more *soigné* and better than I've ever known it to be, but after what you told me, dear friend, I feel *distinctly uncomfortable* when the hour for bye-bye comes!"'

'Pish; what evidence, pray, is that?'

'I regard it as of the very first importance! Sir Trotter admits – a distinguished soldier admits, his uneasiness; and who knows – he is so brave about concealing his woes – his two wives left him! – what he may not have patiently and stoically endured?'

'Less I am sure, my dear, than I of late in listening sometimes to you.'

'I will write, I think, and press him for a more detailed report . . .'

The Ambassador turned away.

'She should no more be trusted with ink than a child with firearms!' he declared, addressing himself with studious indirectness to a garden-snail.

Lady Something blinked.

'Life is a compound,' she murmured again.

'Particularly for women!' the Authoress agreed.

'Ah, well,' the Ambassadress majestically rose, 'I must be off and issue household orders; although I derive hardly my usual amount of enjoyment at present, I regret to say, from my morning consultations with the cook . . .'

XI

It had been once the whim and was now the felicitous habit of the Countess of Tolga to present Count Cabinet annually with a bouquet of flowers. It was as if Venus Anadyomene herself, standing* on a shell and wafted by all the piquant whispers of the town and court, would intrude upon the flattered exile (with her well-wired orchids, and malicious, soulless laughter), to awaken delicate, pagan images of a trecento, Tuscan Greece.

But upon this occasion desirous of introducing some new features, the Countess decided on presenting the fallen senator with a pannier of well-grown, early pears, a small 'heath', and the Erotic Poems, bound in half calf with tasteful tooling, of a Schoolboy Poet, cherishable chiefly perhaps for the vignette frontispiece of the author. Moreover, acting on an impulse she was never able afterwards to explain, she had invited Mademoiselle Olga Blumenghast to accompany her.

Never had summer shown a day more propitiously clement than the afternoon in mid-autumn they prepared to set out.

Fond of a compliment, when not too frankly racy,† and knowing how susceptible the exile was to clothes, the Countess had arrayed herself in a winter gown of kingfisher-tinted silk turning to turquoise, and stencilled in purple at the arms and neck with a crisp Greek-key design; while a voluminous violet veil, depending behind her to a point, half concealed a tricorne turquoise toque from which arose a shaded lilac aigrette branching several ways.

* *Vide* Botticelli.
† In Pisuerga compliments are apt to rival in this respect those of the ardent South.

'I shall probably die with heat, and of course it's most unsuitable; but poor old man, he likes to recall the Capital!' the Countess panted, as, nursing heath, poems and pears, she followed Mademoiselle Olga Blumenghast blindly towards the shore.

Oars, and swaying drying nets, a skyline lost in sun, a few moored craft beneath the little rickety wooden pier awaiting choice:– 'The boatmen, today, darling, seem all so ugly; let's take a sailing-boat and go alone!'

'I suppose there's no danger, darling?' the Countess replied, and scarcely had she time to make any slight objection when the owner of a steady wide-bottomed boat – the *Calypso* – was helping them to embark.

The Island of St Helena, situated towards the lake's bourne, lay distant some two miles or more, and within a short way of the open sea.

With sails distended to a languid breeze the shore eventually was left behind; and the demoiselle cranes, in mid-lake, were able to observe there were two court dames among them.

'Although he's dark, Vi,' Mademoiselle Olga Blumenghast presently exclaimed, dropping her cheek to a frail hand upon the tiller, 'although he's dark, it's odd how he gives one the impression somehow of perfect fairness!'

'Who's that, darling?' the Countess murmured, appraising with fine eyes, faintly weary, the orchid-like style of beauty of her friend.

'Ann-Jules, of course.'

'I begin to wish, do you know, I'd brought pomegranates, and worn something else!'

'What are those big burley-worleys?'

'Pears . . .'

'Give me one.'

'Catch, then.'

'Not that I could bear to be married; especially like *you*, Vi!'

'A marriage like ours, dear, was so utterly unworthwhile . . .'

'I'm not sure, dear, that I comprehend altogether?'

'Seagulls' wings as they fan one's face . . .'

'It's vile and wrong to shoot them: but oh! how I wish your happiness depended, even ever so little, on me.'

The Countess averted her eyes.

Waterfowl, like sadness passing, hovered and soared overhead, casting their dark, fleeting shadows to the white, drowned clouds, in the receptive waters of the lake.

'I begin to wish I'd brought grapes,' she breathed.

'Heavy stodgy pears. So do I.'

'Or a few special peaches,' the Countess murmured, taking up the volume of verse beside her, with a little, mirthless, half-hysterical laugh.

To a Faithless Friend.

To V.O.I. and S.C.P.

For Stephen.

When the Dormitory Lamp burns Low.

Her gaze travelled over the Index.

'Read something, dear,' Mademoiselle Blumenghast begged, toying with the red-shaded flower in her burnished curls.

'Gladly; but oh, Olga!' the Countess crooned.

'What!'

'Where's the wind?'

It had gone.

'We must row.'

There was nothing for it.

To gain the long, white breakwater, with the immemorial willow-tree at its end, that was the most salient feature of the island's approach, required, nevertheless, resolution.

'It's so far, dear,' the Countess kept on saying. 'I had no idea how far it was! Had you any conception at all it was so far?'

'Let us await the wind, then. It's bound to rally.'

But no air swelled the sun-bleached sails, or disturbed the pearly patine of the paralysed waters.

'I shall never get this peace, I only realize it *exists* . . .' the Countess murmured with dream-glazed eyes.

'It's astonishing . . . the stillness,' Mademoiselle Blumenghast murmured, with a faint tremor, peering round towards the shore.

On the banks young censia-trees raised their boughs like strong white whips towards the mountains, upon whose loftier heights lay, here and there, a little stray patch of snow.

'Come hither, ye winds, come hither!' she softly called.

'Oh, Olga! Do we really want it?' the Countess in agitation asked, discarding her hat and veil with a long, sighing breath.

'I don't know, dear; no; not, not much.'

'Nor, I, – at all.'

'Let us be patient then.'

'It's all so beautiful it makes one want to cry.'

'Yes; it makes one want to cry,' Mademoiselle Blumenghast murmured, with a laugh that a brilliance vied with the October sun.

'Olga!'

'So,' as the *Calypso* lurched: 'lend me your hanky, dearest.'

'*Olga* – ? – ? Thou fragile, and exquisite thing!'

. . . .

Meanwhile Count Cabinet was seated with rod-and-line at an open window, idly ogling a swan. Owing to the reluctance of tradespeople to call for orders, the banished statesman was often obliged to supplement the larder himself. But hardly had he been angling ten minutes today when lo! a distinguished mauvish fish with vivid scarlet spots. Pondering on the mysteries of the deep, and of the subtle variety there is in Nature, the veteran ex-minister lit a cigar. Among the more orthodox types that stocked the lake, such as carp, cod, tench, eels, sprats, shrimps, etc., this exceptional fish must have known its trials and persecutions, its hours of superior difficulty . . . and the Count with a stoic smile recalled his own. Musing on the advantages and disadvantages of personality, of 'party' view-points, and of morals in general, the Count was soon too self-absorbed to observe the approach of his 'useful' secretary and amanuensis, Peter Passer.

More valet perhaps than secretary, and more errand-boy than either, the former chorister of the Blue Jesus had followed the fallen statesman into exile at a moment when the Authorities of Pisuerga were making minute inquiries for sundry missing articles,* from the *Trésor* of the Cathedral, and since the strain of constant choir-practice is apt to be injurious for a youngster suffering from a delicate chest, the adolescent had been willing enough to accept, for a time at least, a situation in the country.

'Oh, sir,' he exclaimed, and almost in his excitement forgetting altogether the insidious, lisping tones he preferred as a rule to employ: 'oh, sir, here comes that old piece of rubbish again with a fresh pack of tracts.'

'Collect yourself, Peter, pray do: what, lose our heads for a visit?' the Count said, getting up and going to a glass.

'I've noticed, sir, it's impossible to live on an island long without feeling its effects; you *can't* escape being insular!'

'Or insolent.'

'Insular, sir!'

'No matter much, but if it's the Countess Yvorra you might show her round the garden this time, perhaps, for a change,' the Count replied, adjusting a demure-looking fly, of indeterminate sex, to his line.

And brooding on life and baits, and what *A* will come for while *B* won't, the Count's thoughts grew almost humorous as the afternoon wore on.

Evening was approaching when, weary of the airs of a common carp, he drew in, at length, his tackle.

Like a shawl of turquoise silk the lake seemed to vie, in serenity and radiance, with the bluest day in June, and it was no surprise, on descending presently for a restricted ramble – (the island, in all, amounted to scarcely one acre) – to descry the invaluable Peter enjoying a pleasant swim.

When not boating or reading or feeding his swans, to watch Peter's fancy-diving off the terrace end was perhaps the favourite pastime of the veteran *viveur*: to behold the lad trip along the riven

---

* The missing articles were:—
  5 chasubles.
  A relic-casket in lapis and diamonds, containing the Tongue of St Thelma.
  4¾ yards of black lace, said to have 'belonged to' the Madonna.

breakwater, as naked as a statue, shoot out his arms and spring, the *Flying-head-leap* or the *Backsadilla*, was a beautiful sight, looking up now and again – but more often now – from a volume of old Greek verse; while to hear him warbling in the water with his clear alto voice – of Kyries and Anthems he knew no end – would often stir the old man to the point of tears. Frequently the swans themselves would paddle up to listen, expressing by the charmed or rapturous motions of their necks (recalling to the exile the ecstasies of certain musical or 'artistic' dames at Concert-halls, or the Opera House, long ago) their mute appreciation, their touched delight . . .

'Old goody Two-shoes never came, sir,' Peter archly lisped, admiring his adventurous shadow upon the breakwater wall.

'How is that?'

'Becalmed, sir,' Peter answered, culling languidly a small, nodding rose that was clinging to the wall:

> 'Oh becalmed is my soul,
> I rejoice in the Lord!'

At one extremity of the garden stood the Observatory, and after duly appraising various of Peter's neatest feats the Count strolled away towards it. But before he could reach the Observatory he had first to pass his swans.

They lived, with an ancient water-wheel, beneath a cupola of sun-glazed tiles, sheltered, partially, from the lake by a hedge of towering red geraniums, and the Count seldom wearied of watching these strangely gorgeous creatures as they sailed out and in through the sanguine-hued flowers. A few, with their heads sunk back beneath their wings, had retired for the night already; nevertheless, the Count paused to shake a finger at one somnolent bird, in disfavour for pecking Peter. 'Jealous, doubtless of the lad's grace,' he mused, fumbling with the key of the Observatory door.

The unrivalled instrument that the Observatory contained, whose intricate lenses were capable of drawing even the remote Summer Palace to within an appreciable range, was, like most instruments of merit, sensitive to the manner of its manipulation; and fearing lest the inexpert tampering of a homesick housekeeper (her native village was visible in clear weather, with the aid of a glass) should break or injure the delicate lenses, the Count kept the Observatory usually under key.

But the inclination to focus the mundane and embittered features of the fanatic Countess, as she lectured her boatmen for forgetting their oars, or, being considerably superstitious, to count the moles on their united faces as an esoteric clue to the Autumn Lottery, waned a little before the mystery of the descending night.

Beneath a changing tide of deepening shadow, the lifeless valleys were mirroring to the lake the sombreness of dusk. Across the blue forlornness of the water, a swan, here and there, appeared quite violet, while coiffed in swift, clinging, golden clouds the loftiest hills alone retained the sun.

A faint nocturnal breeze, arising simultaneously with the Angelus-bell, seemed likely to relieve, at the moon's advent, the trials to her patience of the Countess Yvorra: 'who must be cursing,' the Count reflected, turning the telescope about with a sigh, to suit her sail.

Ah poignant moments when the heart stops still! Not since the hour of his exile had the Count's been so arrested.

From the garden Peter's voice rose questingly; but the Count was too wonderstruck, far, to heed it.

Caught in the scarlet radiance of the afterglow, the becalmed boat, for one brief and most memorable second, was his to gaze on.

In certain lands with what diplomacy falls the night, and how discreetly is the daylight gone. Those dimmer-and-dimmer, darker-and-lighter twilights of the North, so disconcerting in their playfulness, were unknown altogether in Pisuerga. There, Night pursued Day as though she meant it. No lingering or arctic sentiment! No concertina-ishness . . . Hard on the sun's heels pressed Night. And the wherefore of her haste; Sun-attraction? Impatience to inherit? An answer to such riddles as these may doubtless be found by turning to the scientist's theories on Time and Relativity.

Effaced in the blue air of evening became everything, and with the darkness returned the wind.

'Sir, sir? . . . Ho, Hi, hiiiiiiiiiiii!!' Peter's voice came again.

But transfixed, and loath just then for company, the Count made no reply.

A green-lanterned barge passed slowly, coming from the sea, and on the mountain-side a village light winked wanly here and there.

'Oh, why was I not *sooner?*' he murmured distractedly aloud.

. . . .

'Oh Olga!'

'Oh Vi!'

'. . . I hope you've enough money for the boat, dear? . . . ?'

'. . . ! ! ?'

'Tell me, Olga: Is my hat all sideways?'

'. . . . .'

The long windows of the Summer Palace were staring white to the moon as the Countess of Tolga, hugging still her heath, her aigrettes casting *heroic* shadows, re-entered the Court's precincts on the arm of her friend.

XII

One evening, as Mrs Montgomery was reading *Vanity Fair* for the fifteenth time, their came a tap at the door. It was not the first interruption since opening the cherished green-bound book, and Mrs Montgomery seemed disinclined to stir. With the Court about to return to winter quarters, and the Summer Palace upside down, the royal governess was still able to command her habitual British phlegm. It had been decided, moreover, that she should remain behind in the forsaken palace with his Naughtiness, the better to 'prepare' him for his forthcoming Eton exam.

Still, with disputes as to the precedence of trunks and dress-baskets simmering in the corridors without, it was easier to enjoy the barley-sugar stick in one's mouth than the novel in one's hand.

'Thank God I'm not touchy!' Mrs Montgomery reflected, rolling her eyes lazily about the little white-wainscoted room.

It was as if something of her native land had crept in through the doorway with her, so successfully had she inculcated its tendencies, or spiritual Ideals, upon everything around.

A solitary teapot, on a bracket, above the door, two *Jubilee* plates, some peacocks' feathers, an image of a little fisher-boy in bathing-drawers with a broken hand, – 'a work of delicate beauty!' – a mezzotint, *The Coiffing of Maria* – these were some of the treasures which the room contained.

'A blessing to be sure when the Court has gone!' she reflected, half rising to drop a curtsey to Prince Olaf who had entered.

'Word from your country,' sententiously he broke out. 'My brother's betrothed! So need I go on with my preparation?'

'Put your tie straight! And just look at your socks all tumbling down. Such great jambons of knees! . . . What will become of you, I ask myself, when you're a lower boy at Eton.'

'How can I be a lower boy when I'm a Prince?'

'Probably the Rev. Ruggles-White, when you enter his House, will be able to explain.'

'I won't be a lower boy! I will *not!*'

'Cs, Cs.'

'Damn the democracy.'

'Fie, sir.'

'Down with it.'

'For shame.'

'Revenge.'

'That will do: and now, let me hear your lessons: I should like,' Mrs Montgomery murmured, her eyes set in detachment upon the floor, 'the present-indicative tense of the Verb *To be!* Adding the words Political h-Hostess; – more for the sake of the pronunciation than for anything else.'

And after considerable persuasion, prompting, and 'bribing' with various sorts of sweets:

> 'I am a Political Hostess,
> Thou art a Political Hostess,
> He is a Political Hostess,
> We are Political Hostesses,
> Ye are Political Hostesses,
> They are Political Hostesses.'

'Very good, dear, and only one mistake. *He* is a Political h-Hostess: can you correct yourself? The error is so slight . . .'

But alas the prince was in no mood for study; and Mrs Montgomery very soon afterwards was obliged to let him go.

Moving a little anxiously about the room, her meditations turned upon the future.

With the advent of Elsie a new régime would be established: increasing Britishers would wish to visit Pisuerga; and it seemed a propitious moment to abandon teaching, and to inaugurate in Kairoulla an English hotel.

'I have no more rooms. I am quite full up!' she smiled, addressing the silver andirons in the grate.

And what a deliverance to have done with instructing unruly children, she reflected, going towards the glass mail-box attached to her vestibule door. Sometimes about this hour there would be a letter in it, but this evening there was only a picture postcard of a field mouse in a bonnet, from her old friend Mrs Bedley.

'We have *Valmouth* at last,' she read, 'and was it you, my dear, who asked for *The Beard Throughout the Ages?* It is in much demand, but I am keeping it back anticipating a *reply*. Several of the plates are missing I see, among them those of the late King Edward and of Assur Bani Pal; I only mention it that you may know I shan't blame you! We are having wonderful weather, and I am keeping pretty well, although poor Mrs Barleymoon, I fear, will not see through another winter. Trusting you are benefiting by the beautiful country air: your obedient servant to command,

ANN BEDLEY.

'P.S. – *Man, and All About Him* is rebinding. Ready I expect soon.'

'Ah! Cunnie, Cunnie . . . ?' Mrs Montgomery murmured, laying the card down near a photograph of the Court-physician with a sigh. 'Ah! Arthur Amos Cuncliffe Babcock . . . ?' she invoked his name dulcetly in full: and, as though in telepathic response, there came a tap at the door, and the doctor himself looked in.

He had been attending, it seemed, the young wife of the Comptroller of the Household at the extremity of the corridor, a creature who, after two brief weeks of marriage, imagined herself to be in an interesting state. '*I believe baby's coming!*' she would cry out every few hours.

'Do I intrude?' he demanded, in his forceful, virile voice, that ladies knew and liked: 'pray say so if I do.'

'Does he intrude!' Mrs Montgomery flashed an arch glance towards the cornice.

'Well, and how are you keeping?' the doctor asked, dropping on to a rep causeuse that stood before the fire.

'I'm only semi-well, doctor, thanks!'

'Why, what's the trouble?'

'You know my organism is not a very strong one, Dr Cuncliffe

. . .' Mrs Montgomery replied, drawing up a chair, and settling a cushion with a sigh of resignation at her back.

'Imagination!'

'If only it were!'

'Imagination,' he repeated, fixing a steady eye on the short train of her black brocaded robe that all but brushed his feet.

'If that's your explanation for continuous broken sleep . . .' she gently snapped.

'Try mescal.'

'I'm trying Dr Fritz Millar's treatment,' the lady stated, desiring to deal a slight *scratch* to his masculine *amour propre*.

'Millar's an Ass.'

'I don't agree at all!' she incisively returned, smiling covertly at his touch of pique.

'What is it?'

'Oh it's horrid. You first of all lie down; and then you drink cold water in the sun.'

'Cold what? I never *heard* of such a thing: it's enough to kill you.'

Mrs Montgomery took a deep-drawn breath of languor.

'And would you care, doctor, so *very* much if it did?' she asked, as a page made his appearance with an ice-bucket and champagne.

'To toast our young Princess!'

'Oh, oh, Dr Cuncliffe? What a wicked man you are.' And for a solemn moment their thoughts went out in unison to the sea-girt land of their birth – Barkers', Selfridge's, Brighton Pier, the Zoological Gardens on a Sunday afternoon.

'Here's to the good old country!' the doctor quaffed.

'The Bride, and,' Mrs Montgomery raised her glass, 'the Old Folks at h-home.'

'The Old Folks at home!' he vaguely echoed.

'Bollinger, you naughty man,' the lady murmured, amiably seating herself on the causeuse at his side.

'You'll find it dull here all alone after the Court has gone,' he observed, smiling down, a little despotically, on to her bright, abundant hair.

Mrs Montgomery sipped her wine.

'When the wind goes whistling up and down under the colonnades: oh, then!' she shivered.

'You'll wish for a fine, bold Pisuergian husband; shan't you?' he answered, his foot drawing closer to hers.

'Often of an evening I feel I need fostering,' she owned, glancing up yearningly into his face.

'Fostering, eh?' he chuckled, refilling with exuberance her glass.

'Why is it that wine always makes me feel *so good?*'

'Probably because it fills you with affection for your neighbour!'

'It's true; I feel I could be very affectionate: I'm what they call an "amoureuse" I suppose, and there it is . . .'

There fell a busy silence between them.

'It's almost too warm for a fire,' she murmured, repairing towards the window; 'but I like to hear the crackle!'

'Company, eh?' he returned, following her (a trifle unsteadily) across the room.

'The night is so clear the moon looks to be almost transparent,' she languorously observed, with a long tugging sigh.

'And so it does,' he absently agreed.

'I adore the pigeons in my wee court towards night, when they sink down like living sapphires upon the stones,' she sentimentally said, sighing languorously again.

'Ours,' he assured her; 'since the surgery looks on to it, too . . .'

'Did you ever see anything so ducky-wucky, so completely twee!' she inconsequently chirruped.

'Allow me to fill this empty glass.'

'I want to go out on all that gold floating water!' she murmured listlessly, pointing towards the lake.

'Alone?'

'Drive me towards the sweet seaside,' she begged, taking appealingly his hand.

'Aggie?'

'Arthur – Arthur, for God's sake!' she shrilled, as with something between a snarl and a roar he impulsively whipped out the light.

'H-Help! Oh Arth –'

Thus did they celebrate the 'Royal engagement'.

XIII

Behind the heavy moucharaby in the little dark shop of Haboubet of Egypt all was song, *fête* and preparation. Additional work had brought additional hands, and be-tarbouched boys, in burnouses, and baskets of blossoms lay strewn all over the floor.

> 'Sweet is the musk-rose of the Land of Punt!
> Sweet are the dates from Khorassân . . .
> But bring *me* (O wandering Djinns) the English rose,
>   the English apple!
> O sweet is the land of the Princess Elsie,
> Sweet indeed is England –'

Bachir's voice soared, in improvisation, to a long-drawn, strident wail.

'Pass me the scissors, O Bachir ben Ahmed, for the love of Allah,' a young man with large lucent eyes and an untroubled face, like a flower, exclaimed, extending a slender, keef-stained land.

'Sidi took them,' the superintendent of the Duchess of Varna replied, turning towards an olive-skinned Armenian youth, who, seated on an empty hamper, was reading to a small, rapt group the *Kairoulla Intelligence* aloud.

'"Attended by Lady Canon-of-Noon and by Lady Bertha Chamberlayne (she is a daughter of Lord Frollo's*) the Princess was seen to alight from her saloon, in a *chic* toque of primrose paille, stabbed with the quill of a nasturtium-coloured bird, and, darting forward, like the Bird of Paradise that she *is*, embraced her future parents-in-law with considerable affection . . ."'

---

* Although the account of Princess Elsie's arrival in Kairoulla is signed 'Green Jersey', it seems not unlikely that 'Eva Schnerb' herself was the reporter on this eventful occasion.

'Scissors, for the love of Allah!'

'"And soon I heard the roll of drums! And saw the bobbing plumes in the jangling browbands of the horses: it was a moment I shall never forget. She passed . . . and as our Future Sovereign turned smiling to bow her acknowledgements to the crowd I saw a happy tear . . . !"'

'Ah Allah.'

'Pass me two purple pinks.'

'"Visibly gratified at the cordial ovation to her Virgin Daughter was Queen Glory, a striking and impressive figure, all a-glitter in a splendid dark dress of nacre and nigger tissue, her many Orders of Merit almost bearing her down."'

'Thy scissors, O Sidi, for the love of Muhammed!'

'"It seemed as if Kairoulla had gone wild with joy. Led by the first Life-Guards and a corps of ladies of great fashion disguised as peasants, the cortège proceeded amid the whole-hearted plaudits of the people towards Constitutional Square, where, with the sweetest of smiles and thanks, the Princess received an exquisite sheaf of Deflas (they are the hybrids of slipper-orchids crossed with maidens-rue, and are all the mode at present), tendered her by little Paula Exelmans, the Lord Mayor's tiny daughter. Driving on, amid showers of confetti, the procession passed up the Chausée, which presented a scene of rare animation; boys and even quite elderly dames swarming up the trees to obtain a better view of their new Princess. But it was not until Lilianthal Street and the Cathedral Square were reached that the climax reached its height! Here a short standstill was called and, after an appropriate address from the Archbishop of Pisuerga, the stirring strains of the National Anthem, superbly rendered by Madame Marguerite Astorra of the State Theatre (she is in perfect voice this season), arose on the air. At that moment a black cat and its kitties rushed across the road, and I saw the Princess smile."'

'Thy scissors, O Sidi, in the Name of the Prophet!'

'"A touching incident,"' Sidi with equanimity pursued, '"was just before the English Tea Rooms, where the English Colony had mustered together in force . . ."'

But alack for those interested. Owing to the clamour about him much of the recital was lost: '"Cheers and tears . . . Life's benison . . . Honiton lace . . . If I live to be *forty*, it was a moment I shall never forget . . . Panic . . . congestion . . . Police."'

But it was scarcely needful to peruse the paper, when on the boulevards outside the festivities were everywhere in full swing. The arrival of the princess for her wedding had brought to Kairoulla unprecedented crowds from all parts of the kingdom, as much eager to see the princess as to catch a glimpse of the fine pack of beagles that it was said had been brought over with her, and which had taken an half-eerie hold of the public mind. Gilderoy, Beausire, Audrey, many of the hounds' names were known pleasantly to the crowd already; and anecdotes of Audrey, picture-postcards of Audrey, were sold as rapidly almost as those even of the princess. Indeed mothers among the people had begun to threaten their disobedient offspring with Audrey, whose silky, thickset frame was supported, it appeared, daily on troublesome little boys and tiresome little girls . . .

'Erri, erri, get on with thy bouquet, oh Lazari Demitraki!' Bachir exclaimed in plaintive tones, addressing a blond boy with a skin of amber, who was 'charming' an earwig with a reed of grass.

'She dance the *Boussadilla* just like in the street of Halfaouine in Gardaïa my town any Ouled Naïl!' he rapturously gurgled.

'Get on with thy work, oh Lazari Demitraki,' Bachir besought him, 'and leave the earwigs alone for the clients to find.'

'What with the heat, the smell of the flowers, the noise of you boys, and with filthy earwigs Boussadillaing all over one, I feel I could *swoon*.' The voice, cracked yet cloying, was Peter Passer's.

He had come to Kairoulla for the 'celebrations', and also, perhaps, aspiring to advance his fortunes, in ways known best to himself. With Bachir his connection dated from long ago, when as a Cathedral choirboy it had been his habit to pin a shoulder- or bosom-blossom to his surplice, destroying it with coquettish, ring-laden fingers in the course of an anthem, and scattering the petals from the choir-loft, leaf by leaf, on to the grey heads of the monsignori below.

'Itchiata wa?' Bachir grumbled, playing his eyes distractedly around the shop. And it might have been better for the numerous orders there were to attend to had he called fewer of his acquaintance to assist him. Sunk in torpor, a cigarette smouldering at his ear, a Levantine Greek known as 'Effendi darling' was listening to a dark-cheeked Tunisian engaged at the Count of Tolga's private Hammam Baths – a young man, who, as he spoke, would make mazy gestures of the hands as though his master's ribs, or those of some illustrious guest, lay under him. But by no means all of those assembled in the little shop bore the seal of Islam. An American, who had grown too splendid for the copper 'Ganymede' or Soda-fountain of a Café bar and had taken to teaching the hectic dance-steps of his native land in the night-halls where Bachir sold, was achieving wonders with some wires and Eucharist lilies, while discussing with a shy-mannered youth the many difficulties that beset the foreigner in Kairoulla.

'Young chaps that come out here don't know what they're coming to,' he sapiently remarked, using his incomparable teeth in place of scissors. 'Gosh! Talk of advancement,' he growled.

'There's few can mix as I can, yet I don't never get no rise!' the shy youth exclaimed, producing a card that was engraved: *Harry Cummings, Salad-Dresser to the King.* 'I expect I've arrived,' he murmured, turning to hide a modest blush towards a pale young man who looked on life through heavy horn glasses.

'Salad dressing? I'd sooner it was hair! You do get tips there anyway,' the Yankee reasoned.

'I wish *I* were – arrived,' the young man with the glasses, by name Guy Thin, declared. He had come out but recently from England to establish a 'British Grocery', and was the owner of what is some-times called an expensive voice, his sedulously clear articulation missing out no syllable or letter of anything he might happen to be saying, as though he were tasting each word, like the Pure tea, or the Pure marmalade, or any other of the so very Pure goods he proposed so exclusively to sell.

'If Allah wish it then you arrive,' Lazari Demitraki assured him with a dazzling smile, catching his hand in order to construe the lines.

'Finish they bouquet, O Lazari Demitraki,' Bachir faintly moaned.

'It finished – arranged: it with Abou!' he announced, pointing to an aged negro with haunted sin-sick eyes who appeared to be making strange grimaces at the wall. A straw hat of splendid dimensions was on his head, flaunting bravely the insignia of the Firm.

But the old man seemed resolved to run no more errands:

'Nsa, nsa,' he mumbled. 'Me walk enough for one day! Me no go out any more. Old Abou too tired to take another single step! as soon would me cross the street again dis night as the Sahara! . . .'

And it was only after the promise of a small gift of Opium that he consented to leave a débutante's bouquet at the Théâtre Diana.*

'In future,' Bachir rose, remarking, 'I only employ the women; I keep only girls,' he repeated, for the benefit of 'Effendi darling' who appeared to be attaining Nirvana.

'And next I suppose you keep a Harem?' 'Effendi darling' somnolently returned.

Most of the city shops had closed their shutters for the day when Bachir, shouldering a pannier bright with blooms, stepped with his companions forth into the street.

Along the Boulevards thousands were pressing towards the Regina Gardens to view the Fireworks, all agog to witness the pack of beagles wrought in brilliant lights due to course a stag across the sky, and which would change, if newspaper reports might be believed, at the critical moment, into '"something of the nature of a surprise".'

Pausing before a plate-glass window that adjoined the shop to adjust the flowing folds of his gandourah, and to hoist his flower tray to his small scornful head, Bachir allowed his auxiliaries to drift, mostly two by two, away among the crowd. Only the royal

---

* The Théâtre Diana: a Music Hall dedicated to Spanish Zarzuelas and Operettes. It enjoyed a somewhat doubtful reputation.

salad-dresser, Harry Cummings, expressed a demure inclination (when the pushing young grocer caressed his arm) to 'be alone'; but Guy Thin, who had private designs upon him, was loath to hear of it! He wished to persuade him to buy a bottle of Vinegar from his Store, when he would print on his paper-bags *As supplied to his Majesty the King.*

'Grant us, O Allah, each good Fortunes,' Bachir beseeched, looking up through his eyelashes towards the moon, that drooped like a silver amulet in the firmament above: in the blue nocturnal air he looked like a purple poppy. 'A toute à l'heure mes amis!' he murmured as he moved away.

And in the little closed shop behind the heavy moucharaby now that they all had gone, the exhalations of the *flowers* arose; pungent, concerted odours, expressive of natural antipathies and feuds, suave alliances, suffering, pride, and joy . . . Only the shining moon through the moucharaby, illumining here a lily, there a leaf, may have guessed what they were saying:

'My wires are hurting me: my wires are hurting me.'

'I have no water. I cannot reach the water.'

'They have pushed me head down into the bottom of the bowl.'

'I'm glad I'm in a Basket! No one will hurl *me* from a window to be bruised underfoot by the callous crowd.'

'It's uncomfy, isn't it, without one's roots?'

'You Weed you! You, you, you . . . *buttercup!* How dare you to *an Orchid!*'

'I shouldn't object to sharing the same water with him, dear . . . ordinary as he is! If *only* he wouldn't smell . . .'

'She's nothing but a piece of common grass and so I tell her!'

Upon the tense pent atmosphere surged a breath of cooler air, and through the street-door slipped the Duchess of Varna.

Overturning a jar of great heavy-headed gladioli with a crash, she sailed, with a purposeful step, towards the till.

Garbed in black and sleepy citrons, she seemed, indeed, to be equipped for a long, long Voyage, and was clutching, in her arms, a pet Poodle dog, and a levant-covered case, in which, doubtless, reposed her jewels.

Since her rupture with Madame Wetme (both the King and Queen had refused to receive her), the money *ennuis* of the Duchess had become increasingly acute. Tormented by tradespeople, dunned and bullied by creditors, menaced, mortified, insulted – an offer to 'star' in the *rôle* of *A Society Thief* for the cinematograph had particularly shocked her – the inevitable hour to quit the Court, so long foreseen, had come. And now with her departure definitely determined upon, the Duchess experienced an insouciance of heart unknown to her assuredly for many a year. Replenishing her reticule with quite a welcome sheaf of the elegant little bank-notes of Pisuerga, one thing only remained to do, and taking pen and paper she addressed to the Editor of the *Intelligence* the supreme announcement:– '*The Duchess of Varna has left for Dateland.*'

Eight light words! But enough to set *tout* Kairoulla in a rustle.

'I only regret I didn't go sooner,' she murmured to herself aloud, breaking herself a rose to match her gown from an arrangement in the window.

Many of the flowers had been newly christened, 'Elsie', 'Audrey', 'London-Madonnas' (black Arums these), while the roses from the 'Land of Punt' had been renamed 'Mrs Lloyd George' – and priced accordingly. A basket of odontoglossums eked out with gypsophila seemed to anticipate the end, when supplies from Punt must necessarily cease. However, bright boys, like Bachir, seldom lacked patrons, and the duchess recalled glimpsing him one evening, from her private sitting-room at the Ritz Hotel, seated on a garden bench in the Regina Gardens beside the Prime Minister himself; both, to all seeming, on the most cordial terms, and having reached a perfect understanding as regards the Eastern Question. Ah, the Eastern Question! It was said that, in the Land of Dates, one might study it well. In Djezira, the chief town, beneath the great golden sun, people, they said, might grow wise. In the simoon that scatters the silver sand, in the words of the nomads, in the fairy mornings beneath the palms, society with its foolish *cliché* . . . the duchess smiled.

'But for that poisonous woman, I should have gone last year,' she told herself, interrupted in her cogitations by the appearance of her maid.

'The train, your Grace, we shall miss it . . .'

'Nonsense!' the duchess answered, following, leaving the flowers alone again to their subtle exhalations.

'I'm glad *I'm* in a Basket!'

'I have no water. I cannot reach the water.'

'Life's bound to be uncertain when you haven't got your roots!'

XIV

On a long-chair, with tired, closed eyes, lay the Queen. Although spared from henceforth the anxiety of her son's morganatic marraige, yet, now that his destiny was sealed, she could not help feeling perhaps he might have done better. The bride's lineage was nothing to boast of – over her great-great-grandparents, indeed, in the year 17—, it were gentler to draw a veil – while, for the rest, disingenuous, undistinguished, more at home in the stables than in a drawing-room, the Queen much feared that she and her future daughter-in-law would scarcely get on.

Yes, the little princess was none too engaging, she reflected, and her poor sacrificed child if not actually trapped . . .

The silken swish of a fan, breaking the silence, induced the Queen to look up.

In waiting at present was the Countess Olivia d'Omptyda, a person of both excellent principles and birth, if lacking, somewhat, in social boldness. Whenever she entered the royal presence she would begin visibly to tremble, which considerably flattered the Queen. Her father, Count 'Freddie' d'Omptyda, an infantile and charming old man, appointed in a moment of unusual vagary Pisuergan Ambassador to the Court of St James's, had lately married a child wife scarcely turned thirteen, whose frivolity and numerous pranks on the high dames of London were already the scandal of the *Corps Diplomatique*.

'Sssh! Noise is the last vulgarity,' the Queen commented, raising a cushion embroidered with raging lions and white uncanny unicorns higher behind her head.

Unstrung from the numerous *fêtes*, she had retired to a distant boudoir to relax, and, having partly disrobed, was feeling remotely Venus of Miloey with her arms half hidden in a plain white cape.

The Countess d'Omptyda furled her fan.

'In this Age of push and shriek . . .' she said and sighed.

'It seems that neither King Geo, nor Queen Glory, *ever* lie down of a day!' her Dreaminess declared.

'Since his last appointment, neither does Papa.'

'The affair of your step-mother and Lady Diana Duff Semour,' the Queen remarked, 'appears to be assuming the proportions of an Incident!'

The Countess dismally smiled. The subject of her step-mother, mistaken frequently for her granddaughter, was a painful one. 'I hear she's like a colt broke loose!' she murmured, dropping her eyes fearfully to her costume.

She was wearing an apron of Parma-violets, and the Order of the Holy Ghost.

'It's a little a pity she can't be more sensible,' the Queen returned, fingering listlessly some papers at her side. Among them was the *Archaeological Society's* initial report relating to the recent finds among the Ruins of Sodom and Gomorrah. From Chedorlahomor came the good news that an *amphora* had been found, from which it seemed that men, in those days, rode sideways, and women straddle-legs, with their heads to the horses' tails, while a dainty cup, ravished from a rock-tomb in the Vale of Akko, ornamented with naked boys and goblets of flowers, encouraged a yet more extensive research.

'You may advance, Countess, with the Archaeologists' report,' the Queen commanded. 'Omitting (skipping, I say) the death of the son of Lord Intriguer.'*

'"It was in the Vale of Akko, about two miles from Sââda,"' the Countess tremblingly began, '"that we laid bare a superb tear-bottle, a unique specimen in *grisaille*, severely adorned with a matron's head. From the inscription there can be no doubt whatever that we have here an authentic portrait of Lot's disobedient, though unfortunate, wife. Ample and statuesque (as the salten image she

---

* The Hon. 'Eddy' Monteith had succumbed: the shock received by meeting a jackal while composing a sonnet had been too much for him. His tomb is in the Vale of Akko, beside the River Dis. Alas, for the *triste* obscurity of his end!

was afterwards to become), the shawl-draped, masklike features are by no means beautiful. It is a face that you may often see today, in down-town 'Dancings', or in the bars of the dockyards or wharves of our own modern cities – Tilbury, 'Frisco, Vera Cruz – a sodden, gin-soaked face that helps to vindicate, if not, perhaps, excuse, the conduct of Lot . . . With this highly interesting example of the Potters' Art was found a novel object, of an unknown nature, likely to arouse, in scientific circles, considerable controversy . . ."'

And just as the lectrice was growing hesitant and embarrassed, the Countess of Tolga, who had the *entrée*, unobtrusively entered the room.

She was looking particularly well in one of the new standing-out skirts ruched with rosebuds, and was showing more of her stockings than she usually did.

'You bring the sun with you!' the Queen graciously exclaimed.

'Indeed,' the Countess answered, 'I ought to apologize for the interruption, but the *poor little thing* is leaving now.'

'What? has the Abbess come?'

'She has sent Sister Irene of the Incarnation instead . . .'

'I had forgotten it was today.'

With an innate aversion for all farewells, yet the Queen was accustomed to perform a score of irksome acts daily that she cordially disliked, and when, shortly afterwards, Mademoiselle de Nazianzi accompanied by a Sister from the Flaming-Hood were announced, they found her quite prepared.

Touched, and reassured at the ex-maid's appearance, the Queen judged, at last, it was safe to unbend. Already very remote and unworldly in her novice's dress, she had ceased, indeed, to be a being there was need any more to either circumvent, humour, or suppress; and now that the threatened danger was gone, her Majesty glanced, half-lachrymosely, about among her personal belongings for some slight token of 'esteem' or *souvenir*. Skimming from cabinet to cabinet, in a sort of hectic dance, she began to fear, as she passed her bibelots in review, that beyond a Chinese Buddha that she believed to be ill-omened, and which for a nun seemed hardly suitable, she could spare nothing about her after all, and in some dilemma she raised her eyes, as though for a crucifix, towards the wall. Above the long-chair a sombre study of a strangled negress in a ditch by Gauguin conjured up today with poignant force a vivid vision of the Tropics.

'The poor Duchess!' she involuntarily sighed, going off into a train of speculation of her own.

Too tongue-tied, or, perhaps, too discreet, to inform the Queen that anything she might select would immediately be confiscated by the Abbess, Sister Irene, while professing her rosary, appraised her surroundings with furtive eyes, crossing herself frequently with a speed and facility due to practice, whenever her glance chanced to alight on some nude shape in stone. Keen, meagre, and perhaps slightly malicious, hers was a curiously pinched face – like a cold violet.

'The Abbess is still in retreat; but sends her duty,' she ventured as the Queen approached a guéridon near which she was standing.

'Indeed? How I envy her,' the Queen wistfully said, selecting, as suited to the requirements of the occasion, a little volume of a mystic trend, the *Cries of Love* of Father Surin,* bound in grey velvet, which she pressed upon the reluctant novice, with a brief, but cordial, kiss of farewell.

'She looked quite pretty!' she exclaimed, sinking to the long-chair as soon as the nuns had gone.

'So like the Cimabue in the long corridor . . .' the Countess of Tolga murmured chillily. It was her present policy that her adored ally, Olga Blumenghast, should benefit by Mademoiselle de Nazianzi's retirement from Court, by becoming nearer to the Queen,when they would work all the wires between them.

'I'd have willingly followed her,' the Queen wearily declared, 'at any rate, until after the wedding.'

'It seems that I and Lord Derbyfield are to share the same closed carriage in the wake of the bridal coach,' the Countess of Tolga said, considering with a supercilious air her rose *suède* slipper on the dark carpet.

* Author of *In the Dusk of the Dawn.*

'He's like some great Bull. What do you suppose he talks about?'

The Countess d'Omptyda repressed a giggle.

'They tell me Don Juan was nothing *nothing* to him . . . He cannot see, he cannot be, oh every hour. It seems he can't help it, and that he simply *has* to!'

'Fortunately Lady Lavinia Lee-Strange will be in the landau as well!'

The Queen laid her cheeks to her hands.

'I all but died, dear Violet,' she crooned, 'listening to an account of her Ancestor, who fell, fighting Scotland, at the battle of Pinkie Cleugh.'

'These well-bred, but detestably insular women, how they bore one.'

'They are not to be appraised by any ordinary standards. Crossing the state saloon while coming here what should I see, ma'am, but Lady Canon of Noon on her hands and knees (all fours!) peeping below the loose-covers of the chairs in order to examine the Gobelins-tapestries beneath . . .'

'Oh –'

'"Absolutely authentic," I said, as I passed on, leaving her looking like a pickpocket caught in the act.'

'I suppose she was told to make a quiet survey . . .'

'Like their beagles and deer-hounds, that their Landseer so loved to paint, I fear the British character is, at bottom, *nothing* if not rapacious!'

'It's said, I believe, that to behold the Englishman at his *best* one should watch him play tip-and-run.'

'You mean of course cricket?'

The Queen looked doubtful: she had retained of a cricket-match at Lord's a memory of hatless giants waving wooden sticks.

'I only wish it could have been a long engagement,' she abstrusely murmured, fastening her attention on the fountains whitely spurting in the gardens below.

Valets in cotton jackets and light blue aprons, bearing baskets of crockery and *argenterie*, were making ready beneath the tall Tuba trees a supper *buffet* for the evening's Ball.

'Flap your wings, little bird,
Oh flap your wings –'

A lad's fresh voice, sweet as a robin's, came piping up.

'These wretched workpeople –! There's not a peaceful corner,' the Queen complained, as her husband's shape appeared at the door. He was followed by his first secretary – a simple commoner, yet with the air and manner peculiar to the husband of a Countess.

'Yes, Willie? I've a hundred headaches. What is it?'

'Both King Geo and Queen Glory are wondering where you are.'

'Oh, really, Willie?'

'And dear Elsie's asking after you too.'

'Very likely,' the Queen returned with quiet complaisance, 'but unfortunately, I have neither her energy nor,' she murmured with a slightly sardonic laugh, 'her appetite!'

The Countess of Tolga tittered.

'She called for fried-eggs and butcher's-meat, this morning, about the quarter before eight,' she averred.

'An excellent augury for our dynasty,' the King declared, reposing the eyes of an adoring grandparent upon an alabaster head of a Boy attributed to Donatello.

'She's terribly foreign, Willie . . . ! Imagine ham and eggs . . .' The Queen dropped her face to her hand.

'So long as the Royal-House –' The King broke off, turning gallantly to raise the Countess d'Omptyda, who had sunk with a gesture of exquisite allegiance to the floor.

'Sir . . . Sir!' she faltered in confusion, seeking with fervent lips her Sovereign's hand.

'What is she doing, Willie!'

'Begging for Strawberry-leaves!' the Countess of Tolga brilliantly commented.

'Apropos of Honours . . . it appears King Geo has signified his intention of raising his present representative in Pisuerga to the peerage.'

'After her recent *Cause*, Lady Something should be not a little consoled.'

'She was at the début of the new diva, little Miss Helvellyn (the foreign invasion had indeed begun!), at the Opera-House last night, so radiant . . .'

'When she cranes forward out of her own box to smile at someone into the next, I can't explain . . . but one feels she ought to hatch,' the Queen murmured, repairing capriciously from one couch to another.

'We neglect our guests, my dear,' the King expostulatingly exclaimed, bending over his consort anxiously from behind.

'Tell me, Willie,' she cooed, caressing the medals upon his breast, and drawing him gently down: 'tell me. Didst thou enjoy thy cigar, dear, with King Geo?'

'I can recall in my time, Child, a suaver flavour . . .'

'Thy little chat, though, dearest, was well enough?'

'I would not call him crafty, but I should say he was a man of considerable subtlety . . .' the King evasively replied.

'One does not need, my dearest nectarine, a prodigy of intelligence, however, to take him in!'

'Before the proposed Loan, love, can be brought about, he may wish to question thee as to thy political opinions.'

The Queen gave a little light laugh.

'No one knows what my political opinons are; I don't myself!'

'And I'm quite confident of it: But, indeed, my dear, we neglect our functions.'

'I only wish it could have been a *long* engagement, Willie . . .'

XV

In the cloister eaves the birds were just awakening, and all the spider scales, in the gargoyled gables, glanced fresh with dew. Above the Pietà on the porter's gate, slow-speeding clouds, like knots of pink roses, came blowing across the sky, sailing away in titanic bouquets towards the clear horizon. All virginal in the early sunrise, what enchantment the world possessed! The rhythmic sway-sway of the trees, the exhalations of the flowers, the ethereal candour of this early hour, – these raised the heart up to their Creator.

Kneeling at the casement of a postulant's cell, Laura de Nazianzi recalled that serene, and just thus, had she often planned must dawn her bridal day!

Beyond the cruciform flower-beds and the cloister wall soared the Blue Jesus, the storied windows of its lofty galleries aglow with light.

'Most gracious Jesus. Help me to forget. For my heart aches. Uphold me now.'

But to forget today was well-nigh, she knew, impossible . . .

Once it seemed she caught the sound of splendid music from the direction of the Park, but it was too early for music yet. Away in the palace the Princess Elsie must be already astir . . . in her peignoir, perhaps? The bridal-garment unfolded upon the bed: but no; it was said the bed indeed was where usually her Royal-Highness's dogs . . .

With a long and very involuntary sigh, she began to sweep, and put in some order, her room.

How forlorn her cornette looked upon her *prie-Dieu!* And, oh, how stern, and 'old'!

Would an impulse to bend it slightly, but only so, *so* slightly, to an angle to suit her face, be attended, later, by remorse?

'Confiteor Deo omnipotenti, beatae Mariae semper virgini, beato

Michaeli Archangelo (et *tibi* Pater), quia peccavi nimis cogitatione, verbo et opere,' she entreated, reposing her chin in meditation upon the handle of her broom.

The bluish shadow of a cypress-tree on the empty wall fascinated her as few pictures had.

'Grant my soul eyes,' she prayed, cheerfully completing her task.

It being a general holiday, all was yet quite still in the corridor. A sound as of gentle snoring came indeed from behind more than one closed door, and the new *pensionnaire* was preparing to beat a retreat when she perceived, in the cloister, the dumpish form of Old Jane.

Seated in the sun by the convent well, the Porteress was sharing a scrap of breakfast with the birds.

'You're soonish for Mass, love,' she broke out, her large archaic features surcharged with smiles.

'It's such a perfect morning, I felt I must come down.'

'I've seen many a more promising sunrise before now, my dear, turn to storm and blast! An orange sky overhead brings back to me the morning that I was received; ah, I shall never forget, as I was taking my Vows, a flash of forked lightning, and a clap of Thunder (Glory be to God!), followed by a waterspout (Mercy save us!) bursting all over my French lace veil . . .'

'What is your book, Old Jane?'

'Something light, love, as it's a holiday.'

'*Pascal* . . .'

'Though it's mostly a *Fête* day I've extra to do!' the Porteress averred, dropping her eyes to the great, glistening spits upon the Cloister flags. It was her boast she could distinguish Monsignor Pott's round splash from Father Geordie Picpus's more dapper fine one, and again the Abbess's from Mother Martinez de la Rosa's — although these indeed shared a certain opaque sameness.

'Of course it's a day for private visits.'

'Since the affair of Sister Dorothea and Brother Bernard Soult, private visits are no longer allowed,' the Porteress returned, reproving modestly, with the cord of her discipline, a pert little lizard, that seemed to be proposing to penetrate between the nude toes of her sandalled foot.

But on such a radiant morning it was preposterous to hint at 'Rules'.

Beneath the clement sun a thousand cicadas were insouciantly chirping, while birds, skimming about without thoughts of money, floated lightly from tree to tree.

'Jesus – Mary – Joseph!' the Porteress purred, as a Nun, with her face all muffled up in wool, crossed the Cloister, glancing neither to right nor left, and sharply slammed a door: for, already, the Convent was beginning to give signs of animation. Deep in a book of Our Lady's Hours, a biretta'd priest was slowly rounding a garden path, while repairing from a *Grotto-sepulchre*, to which was attached a handsome indulgence, Mother Martinez de la Rosa appeared, all heavily leaning on her stick.

Simultaneously the matin-bell rang out, calling all to prayer.

The Convent Chapel, founded by the tender enthusiasm of a wealthy widow, the Countess d'Acunha, to perpetuate her earthly comradeship with the beautiful Andalusian, the Doña Dolores Baatz, was still but thinly peopled some few minutes later, although the warning bell had stopped.

Peering around, Laura was disappointed not to remark Sister Ursula in her habitual place, between the veiled fresco of the 'Circumcision' and the stoup of holy-water by the door.

Beyond an offer to 'exchange whippings' there had been a certain coolness in the greeting with her friend that had both surprised and pained her.

'When those we rely on wound and betray us, to whom should we turn but Thee?' she breathed, addressing a crucifix, in ivory, contrived by love, that was a miracle of wonder.

Finished Mass, there was a general rush for the Refectory!

Preceded by Sister Clothilde, and followed, helter-skelter, by an exuberant bevy of nuns, even Mother Martinez, who, being short-sighted, would go feeling the ground with her cane, was propelled to the measure of a hop-and-skip.

Passing beneath an archway labelled 'Silence' (the injunction today being undoubtedly ignored), the company was welcomed by the mingled odours of tea, *consommé*, and fruit. It was a custom of the Convent for one of the Sisters during meal-time to read aloud from some standard work of fideism, and these edifying recitations, interspersed by such whispered questions as: 'Tea, or *Consommé?*' 'A Banana, or a Pomegranate?' gave to those at all foolishly or hysterically inclined a painful desire to giggle. Mounting the pulpit-lectern, a nun with an aristocratic though gourmand little face was about to resume the arid life of the Byzantine monk, Basilius Saturninus, when Mother Martinez de la Rosa took it upon herself, in a few patriotic words, to relax all rules for that day.

'We understand in the world now,' a little faded woman murmured to Laura upon her right, 'that the latest craze among ladies is to gild their tongues; but I should be afraid,' she added diffidently, dipping her banana into her tea, 'of poison, myself!'

Unhappy at her friend's absence from the Refectory, Laura, however, was in no mood to entertain the nuns with stories of the present pagan tendencies of society.

Through the bare, blindless windows, framing a sky so bluely luminous, came the swelling clamour of the assembling crowds, tinging the languid air as with some sultry fever. From the *Chausée*, music of an extraordinary intention – heated music, crude music, played with passionate élan to perfect time, conjured up, with vivid, heartrending prosaicness, the seething Boulevards beyond the high old creeper-covered walls.

'I forget now, Mother, which of the Queens it is that will wear a velvet train of a beautiful orchid shade; but one of them will!' Sister Irene of the Incarnation was holding forth.

'I must confess,' Mother Martinez remarked, who was peeling herself a peach, with an air of far attention, 'I must confess, I should have liked to have cast my eye upon the *lingerie* . . .'

'I would rather have seen the ball-wraps, Mother, or the shoes, and evening slippers!'

'Yes, or the fabulous jewels . . .'

'Of course Sister Laura saw the *trousseau?*'

But Laura made feint not to hear.

Discipline relaxed, a number of nuns had collected provisions and were picnicking in the window, where Sister Innez (an ex-Repertoire actress) was giving some spirited renderings of her chief successful parts – *Jane de Simerose, Frou-Frou, Sappho, Cigarette . . .*

'My darling child! I always sleep all day and only revive when there's *a Man*,' she was saying with an impudent look, sending the scandalized Sisters into delighted convulsions.

Unable to endure it any longer, Laura crept away.

A desire for air and solitude led her towards the Recreation ground. After the hot refectory, sauntering in the silken shade of the old astounding cedars was delightful quite. In the deserted alleys, the golden blossoms of the censia-trees, unable to resist the sun, littered in perfumed piles the ground, overcoming her before long with a sensation akin to *vertige*. Anxious to find her friend, Laura turned towards her cell.

She found Sister Ursula leaning on her window-ledge all crouched up – like a Duchess on 'a First Night'.

'My dear, my dear, the *crowds!*'

'Ursula?'

'Yes, what is it?'

'Perhaps I'll go, since I'm in the way.'

'Touchy Goose,' Sister Ursula murmured, wheeling round with a glance of complex sweetness.

'Ah, Ursula,' Laura sighed, smiling reproachfully at her friend.

She had long almond eyes, one longer and larger than the other, that gave to her narrow, etiolated face an exalted, mystic air. Her hair, wholly concealed by her full coif, would be inclined to rich copper or chestnut: indeed, below the pinched and sensitive nostrils, a moustache (so slight as to be scarcely discernible) proved this beyond all controversy to be so. But perhaps the quality and beauty of her hands were her chief distinction.

'Do you believe it would cause an earthquake if we climbed out, dear little one, upon the leads?' she asked.

'I had forgotten you overlooked the street by leaning out,' Laura answered, sinking fatigued to a little cane armchair.

'Listen, Laura . . . !'

'This cheering racks my heart . . .'

'Ah, Astaroth! There went a very "swell" carriage.'

'Perhaps I'll come back later: it's less noisy in my cell.'

'Now you're here, I shall ask you, I think, to whip me.'

'Oh, no . . .'

'Bad dear Little-One. Dear meek soul.' Sister Ursula softly laughed.

'This maddening cheering,' Laura breathed, rolling tormented eyes about her.

A crucifix, a text, *I would lay Pansies at Jesus' Feet*, two fresh eggs in a blue paper bag, some ends of string, a breviary, and a birch were the chamber's individual if meagre contents.

'You used *not* to have that text, Ursula,' Laura observed, her attention arrested by the preparation of a Cinematograph Company on the parapet of the Cathedral.

The Church had much need indeed of Reformation! The Times were incredibly low. A new crusade . . . she ruminated, revolted at the sight of an old man holding dizzily to a stone-winged angel, with a wine-flask at his lips.

'Come, dear, won't you assist me now to mortify my senses?' Sister Ursula cajoled.

'No, really, no –! –! –!'

'Quite lightly. For I was scourged, by Sister Agnes, but yesterday, with a heavy bunch of keys, head downwards, hanging from a bar.'

'Oh . . .'

'This morning she sent me those pullets' eggs. I perfectly was touched by her delicate sweet sympathy.'

Laura gasped.

'It must have hurt you?'

'I assure you I felt nothing – my spirit had travelled so far,' Sister Ursula replied, turning to throw an interested glance at the street.

It was close now upon the critical hour, and the plaudits of the crowd were becoming more and more uproarious, as 'favourites' in

Public life and 'celebrities' of all sorts began to arrive in brisk succession at the allotted door of the Cathedral.

'I could almost envy the fleas in the Cardinal's vestments,' Sister Ursula declared, overcome by the venal desire to see.

Gazing at the friend upon whom she had counted in some disillusion, Laura quietly left her.

The impulse to witness something of the spectacle outside was, nevertheless, infectious, and recollecting that from the grotto-sepulchre in the garden it was not impossible to attain the convent wall, she determined, moved by some wayward instinct, to do so. Frequently, as a child, had she scaled it, to survey the doings of the city streets beyond – the streets named by the nuns often 'Sinward-ho'. Crossing the cloisters, and through old gates crowned by vast fruit-baskets in stone, she followed, feverishly, the ivy-masked bricks of the sheltering wall, and was relieved to reach the grotto without encountering anyone. Surrounded by heavy boskage, it marked a spot where once long ago one of the Sisters, it was said, had received the mystic stigmata . . . With a feline effort (her feet supported by the grotto boulders), it needed but a bound to attain an incomparable post of vantage.

Beneath a blaze of bunting, the street seemed paved with heads. 'Madonna,' she breathed, as an official on a white horse, its mane stained black, began authoritatively backing his steed into the patient faces of the mob below, startling an infant in arms to a frantic fit of squalls.

'Just so shall we stand on the Day of Judgement,' she reflected, blinking at the glare.

Street boys vending programmes, 'lucky' horseshoes, Saturn-alian emblems (these for gentlemen only), offering postcards of 'Geo and Glory,' etc., wedged their way, however, where it might have been deemed indeed impossible for anyone to pass.

And *he*, she wondered, her eyes following the wheeling pigeons, alarmed by the recurrent salutes of the signal guns, he must be there already: under the dome! restive a little beneath the busy scrutiny, his tongue like the point of a blade . . .

A burst of cheering seemed to announce the Queen. But no, it was only a lady with a parasol sewn with diamonds that was exciting the rah-rahs of the crowd. Followed by mingled cries of 'Shame!' 'Waste!' and sighs of envy, Madame Wetme was enjoying a belated triumph. And now a brief lull, as a brake containing various delegates and 'representatives of English Culture', rolled by at a stately trot – Lady Alexander, E. V. Lucas, Robert Hichens, Clutton Brock, etc., – the ensemble the very apotheosis of worn-out *cliché*.

'There's someone there wot's got enough heron plumes on her head!' a young girl in the crowd remarked.

And nobody contradicted her.

Then troops and outriders, and at last the Queen.

She was looking charming in a Corinthian chlamyde, in a carriage lined in deep delphinium blue, behind six restive blue roan horses.

Finally, the bride and her father, bowing this way and that . . .

Cheers.

'Huzzas . . .'

A hushed suspense.

Below the wall the voice of a beggar arose, persistent, haunting: 'For the Love of God . . . In the Name of Pity . . . of Pity.'

'Of Pity,' she echoed, addressing a frail, wind-sown harebell, blue as the sky: and leaning upon the shattered glass ends, that crowned the wall, she fell to considering the future – obedience – solitude – death.

The troubling *valse* theme from *Dante in Paris* interrupted her meditations.

How often had they valsed it together, he and she . . . sometimes as a two-step . . . ! What souvenirs . . . Yousef, Yousef . . . Above the Cathedral, the crumbling clouds had eclipsed the sun. In the intense meridian glare the thronged street seemed even as though half-hypnotized; occasionally only the angle of a parasol would change, or some bored soldier's legs would give a little. When brusquely, from the belfry, burst a triumphant clash of bells.

Laura caught her breath.

Already?

A shaking of countless handkerchiefs in wild ovation: from

roof-tops, and balconies, the air was thick with falling flowers – the bridal pair!

But only for the bridegroom had she eyes.

Oblivious of what she did, she began to beat her hands, until they streamed with blood, against the broken glass ends upon the wall: 'Yousef, Yousef, Yousef . . .'

July 1921, May 1922.
Versailles, Montreux, Florence.